THE GIRL IN BETWEEN

o one I'm invisible. I'm sees m
es I'm inv. No one sees invisible
ne. isible. me. I'm invisible. No one see
I'm one sees me. I'm inv
nvisible. No I'm invisible. No isible
o one sees no one sees me. one
I'm invi me. I'm invisible. sees me.
o one sible. No one sees me. I'm
sees me. No one invisible.
I'm I'm invisible no one sees. sees me. I'm
nvis. No one sees. I'm invisible
le. No one sees me. I'm invisible
m invisible. invisible. I'm inv
o one I'm inv. no one sees isible
ees me. isible. I'm invi
m invisible. No one
o one I'm
ees visible

No one I'm invisible. I'm sees me. No one sees me. I'm invisible. No one sees me. I'm invisible. No one sees me. I'm invisible. No one sees me. I'm invisible. No one sees me. I'm invisible. No one sees me. I'm invisible. No one sees me. I'm invisible. No one sees me. I'm invisible. No one sees me.

THE

GIRL

IN

BETWEEN

SARAH CARROLL

SIMON & SCHUSTER

First published in Great Britain in 2017 by Simon & Schuster UK Ltd
A CBS COMPANY

1 3 5 7 9 10 8 6 4 2

Simon & Schuster UK Ltd
1st Floor, 222 Gray's Inn Road
London WC1X 8HB

www.simonandschuster.co.uk
www.simonandschuster.com.au
www.simonandschuster.co.in

Simon & Schuster Australia, Sydney
Simon & Schuster India, New Delhi

A CIP catalogue record for this book
is available from the British Library.

PB ISBN 978-1-4711-6062-2
eBook ISBN 978-1-4711-6063-9

This book is a work of fiction. Names, characters, places
and incidents are either the product of the author's imagination or
are used fictitiously. Any resemblance to actual people living
or dead, events or locales is entirely coincidental.

Typeset in the UK by M Rules
Printed and bound by CPI Group (UK) Ltd, Croydon, CR0 4YY

Simon & Schuster UK Ltd are committed to sourcing paper
that is made from wood grown in sustainable forests and support the Forest
Stewardship Council, the leading international forest certification organisation.
Our books displaying the FSC logo are printed on FSC certified paper.

For Bob, for believing in me,
And for Fiadh, for bringing this novel
into the world with you

PART

ONE

BEGGING

I'm invisible. Ma says I'm supposed to be so the Authorities don't get me. She goes out into the streets almost every day but I'm not allowed. I've got to stay inside the mill so they don't see me. When she's going she says, 'Stay away from the roof, it's a bleeding deathtrap. And don't go near them windows neither. And don't even think of leaving this building or I'll lose ye and I'll never find ye again.'

Me and Ma are begging outside the mill. I'm by the door in the shadow where no one can see me. This is as far as I'm allowed to go. Ma's out on the bottom step.

'Spare change, mister?' Ma asks a man. But I can tell from the way Ma says it that she doesn't really care. She'd rather be in the backyard sunbathing.

It's a sunny day, which means good and bad news for begging. Good news cos we're not getting wet and people are happy. Bad news cos people always give more when it's raining. They feel sorry for us cos they think we sleep out on the streets. They don't know that we don't do that any more. They don't realize that the mill is our Castle and we're safe in here.

'Any spare change?' Ma calls. There's a woman walking past her who pretends like she's heard nothing.

Ma flicks back her hair and ties it into a ponytail that reaches halfway down her back. She pulls out the front of the top she's wearing and blows on her chest to try to cool down. The pointy parts of her shoulders are all shiny from sweat and she wipes them with her hands.

Ma's real pointy. She has a pointy nose and pointy ears. Her elbows and knees are all knobbly too. She used to be much pointier, though, back when we lived on the streets.

She's real short. I'm almost as tall as her. But I'm not pointy. Ma says I've got a head like a basketball. That's why I'm so smart, she says. Cos my head's so big.

Ma says I take after me da. But I wouldn't know.

She picks up the begging cup and rattles it.

'Do we have enough, Ma?' I say.

'Nah, not if I'm getting batteries today too.' She puts it down and leans forwards and looks down the street. Then she rubs the sweat off her hands on her jeans and watches the people passing again.

Ma calls the mill a poxy hole. She says she doesn't know how we got stuck here. But I call it the Castle. It's the biggest place we've ever stayed and I think it's the best, even though it has boards covering some of the broken windows and weeds growing in between the big stones in the walls and the top three floors are so rotted that you can't run across the middle of the rooms. You have to keep close to the wall and go real slow and be ready to jump if the wood breaks, cos if you fall through, you'll break your neck.

Ma says it's a deathtrap. But that doesn't scare me cos if you fall, you just hurt yourself a bit, that's all.

'Spare change?' Ma asks a woman who's walking along smiling at nothing. She must've been daydreaming and didn't see Ma sitting on the doorstep, cos she jumps back a bit and almost trips off the kerb into the road.

'Sorry, I've got nothing,' she says, and starts walking real fast, but even I can see from back here that her purse is bulging.

'I'm bored,' Ma says. Then she says, 'Jaysus, it's hot for September.'

The sun is so high that it's right in the middle of the buildings, shining down the street. I can't even look at the offices across the road cos they're all glass, and the way the sun hits the windows is like daggers in my brain.

'Think I'll work on me tan,' I say, and I roll up my sleeves like the way Ma does and start shuffling out the doorway. But as soon as the sun hits my face, I wish I'd stayed where I was, cos I don't want to be seen and grabbed by the Authorities again. I'm never leaving the mill, not till I'm grown and have a house like Gran's to go to.

Ma sees me. 'Get back in there, you,' she says in a real low voice.

'Ah, Ma, they can't see me, I'm invisible,' I say, but I'm already creeping backwards.

Ma gives me this look, like she's sucking an egg, so I move quicker. I'm back in the shadow, hidden again. But she keeps staring at me so I look at the ground and say nothing, cos she's angry with me and I don't know why. Maybe it's cos I said I'm invisible. Maybe 'invisible' is a new Stress Word.

Some words I say, Ma tells me to shut up cos I'm stressing her out. And when Ma's stressed it means it's time to move on. I've got to go with her cos no matter what happens, I always go with Ma. Ma never leaves me behind. Except for that one time a year and eight months ago when the Authorities almost grabbed me in the alleyway. But she was real sorry after, and she promised then that we'd never sleep on the streets again and I'd never be scared again and she'd never, ever drink again. And she hasn't.

In the Castle, Ma's been good. And nothing stresses me out and I'm never scared. Not any more. The Castle is safe. The Authorites don't know I'm here. And no one else can get in.

I hope Ma's not mad now cos I don't want her stressed out. I wait another bit and then I look up. She's still staring at me, but then she sighs and says, 'You? Invisible? Sure you can be heard a mile off.' She turns back to the street and I smile cos she's not mad and she's not sad neither, so it's all okay.

When Ma was sad, it was the worst kind of stressed out. Her eyes would go all deep, as deep as the canal that runs past the mill. She'd just sit in a doorway begging and not saying anything, and when she had enough change we'd get up and I'd have to run cos Ma would be walking real fast and her arms would be pumping like she wanted to punch someone.

We'd go to the gate, the black one with the evil smiley face. That's where Ma went to buy what she needed. And then we'd go find a doorway where no one could see us.

I'm not stupid. I knew what she was doing. I knew what she was taking. She'd say, 'It's just for the stress, love. It helps me to fly over the city,' which is dumb cos she didn't go anywhere. She just lay there like she was dead.

But her eyes haven't looked as deep as that in ages. And I try to remember not to say things that make her mad or things that make her sad. Like talking about Gran's house. Or my old school. Or her old mates. Or anything from our old life really. And I never, ever talk about that night in the alleyway.

And from now on I'd better remember not to say I'm invisible neither.

'Bored,' Ma says again and then she says something else but I don't hear her cos there's a loud bang from the construction site across the road. You can't see it from here – it's behind the glass building – but from the roof you can watch the cranes lifting massive metal bars and concrete blocks. There are loads of cranes, these days, and loads of new buildings too. Everything is new. The cranes eat the old buildings and put up new ones that all have perfect windows and perfect corners and all look the exact same. The mill is the only one that's not shiny and packed with millions of people typing on computers.

Ma says the mill is useless but I don't think it is. The new buildings are like empty notebooks. But the mill is like a book with pictures. It has a story. And even I don't know the whole story and I've lived here for one year and eight months.

I know the mill has a story cos there's something strange going on.

I was playing a game last week where I was a princess in a forest leaving a trail of coins for an evil witch to follow. I left them all over the bottom three floors of the Castle. And they just disappeared. When I went back to get them, they were gone.

Then that night I heard this shuffling sound when me and Ma were in bed and the whole place was locked up. This part of the city is dead quiet at night, cos all the office workers have marched off home and there's hardly any traffic on the road. So the tiniest sound in the Castle booms through it till you feel it rattle and shake, like when a big truck drives over the canal bridge.

I know I heard something.

I've decided that I'm going to find out what it is later today when Ma leaves. Cos even if it's scary, we live here and we're never leaving. So if there's something going on inside, I need to know.

But I need to get rid of Ma first and she won't go out till she has enough coins.

There's a man getting out of a taxi. He grabs his suitcase and slams the door and starts walking our way.

'Point Blank,' I say.

'Definitely,' Ma says.

Everyone ignores Ma. But if she asks for change, then there are four types of people:

Sorry Nothings – the ones that look real embarrassed and say, 'Sorry, nothing.'

Fake Smiles – the ones that root around for change and give Ma a fake smile when they're throwing it in her cup.

Runners – the ones that put coins in her cup without looking at her and then get out of here like their shoes are on fire.

Point Blanks – the ones that ignore her like she's invisible.

Most people are Point Blanks, like this man. He spots Ma from a few metres back. He pulls up his sleeve and stares at his watch.

'Spare change?' Ma asks, but what she's really saying is 'I know you can see me.'

But he must have bad eyesight, cos he lifts his arm real close to his face and stares at his watch till he's well past us.

'Stingy git,' Ma says.

'Here, Ma,' I say. 'Why don't you ask them for spare change as if you were asking them what's forty-seven times sixty-two?'

Ma turns and gives me a look. She knows I hate maths but it's her favourite subject to teach me and she thinks I'm messing with her so I say, 'Go on,' and I nod at a woman who's coming our way pushing a buggy.

When she's coming past the steps, Ma says, 'Any spare change?' in this real confused way, and it sounds so weird that the woman actually stops and thinks about it and nods like she reckons it's a fair enough question and drops some money into the cup.

I let out a whoop and then slap a hand over my mouth, cos I don't think the woman would be happy about me cheering. But she didn't notice me. Ma turns and gives me a wink.

Now there's a young guy coming, but he's got his face stuck in his phone and he's definitely a Point Blank. Behind him is another man and he's dressed in tight jeans and a shirt with loads of squares on it, and he has a beard that looks more like it was painted on than it grew there.

'Ma, ask him like you're remembering something deadly that happened years ago.'

When he gets close, Ma says, 'You wouldn't have any spare change, would you?' She says it in this voice like melted ice cream and he gives her a weird smile. Ma's pretty good-looking. Especially now that she's not dying from the drink any more. Men are always her best customers.

He actually stops walking, grabs a handful of change and puts it in the cup without even counting it. Ma laughs. And so do I, cos I think we've just found a new type.

'Fair play to ye,' she says.

'Not a bother,' he says.

She turns to me and she's smiling. Really smiling.

'You're a genius!' she says and I'm smiling too.

For the next half hour no one gives any more change, except for an old woman and I feel bad about that cos she looks like she needs it more than we do.

It's boring again and Ma reckons we have enough coins now. I can't see into the cup but I think we probably do.

Ma needs coins to buy food and batteries, but I need coins today too so I can find out what's going on in the Castle. But Ma can't know. I don't want to do anything that'd stress her out. So I'll have to nick some when she's not looking and figure it out on my own.

I notice another man coming. He's in a tight blue suit and his hair looks like the canal does today. Real sleek.

'Look at the head on him. Loves himself,' I say. Ma agrees. Then I say, 'Ma, why don't you ask him like you're telling him to watch out for a truck that's about to hit him?'

I don't think she's going to. I'm not even sure she's heard me. But then just as he clip-clops past us, Ma roars, 'Spare change?'

He jumps and I jump and Ma doesn't move. He curses under his breath and then runs away like Ma's pointing a gun at him. I break my heart laughing.

But then Ma turns her head and I see the look on her face. She's not laughing. Not one bit. She's watching something further down the street.

I lean forwards and I don't know what she's seen at first but then my stomach flips. Before I even figure out what it is, I'm jumping up. Neon yellow jackets.

11

'The Authorities,' I say.

There are two men in yellow jackets. One of them is holding a roll of paper and the other takes one end and pulls it out till they're holding a huge sheet between them. They look at the paper and then up at the mill and then down at the paper again. Now one of them is drawing a line on the sheet with his finger and then pointing upward at the mill and drawing a line through the air. The other one is nodding and looking and nodding.

My heart starts going mental. I can't move. I'm stuck.

It's them.

And I remember the smell of rotting vegetables in the alleyway the night Ma left me alone. The air was so cold it stung to breathe. The Yellow Jackets came to take me away. I was on my own and I was so scared and Ma wasn't there.

But then she was.

'Ma?' I whisper.

She ignores me.

'Ma?'

She's just staring at them and I can't hardly breathe.

'Ma!' I say. I'm pushing the door open when she finally remembers me, and she whips round and points behind me and says, 'Inside, you, now!'

But by the time she says it, I'm already inside, hidden in the darkness of the basement.

NESTING

I wait for Ma to close the door and I can't hardly see cos it was so bright outside and it's so dark in here.

'Ma, what are the Authorities doing out there?' All I can think about is the blue light bouncing off the walls of the alleyway.

'I dunno,' she says. She's biting her nails.

I start to breathe real hard.

Ma notices. 'What's—' she says but then she cops on what's wrong with me. 'No, ye eejit. They're not . . .' She stops whatever she was saying and she looks at me like she's trying to think of the best words to use. 'It's nothing to do with you, love.' She hugs me in a big bear hug. Then she pushes me away and holds my shoulders and looks straight at me and she says, 'I mean it. It's all grand. They're not looking for you. Okay?'

I don't say anything but I'm starting to breathe normal

again. I've bitten my cheek. I taste blood in my mouth. I lick the rough patch of skin and then stick my tongue out, going all cross-eyed trying to see the blood in the dark.

Ma smiles at me and says, 'They were looking at a map, weren't they?' She waits until I nod. 'They were lost, that's all. They're probably already gone. Okay?' She keeps holding my shoulders and trying to look me in the eye. 'Okay?' she says again.

I nod. 'Okay,' I say.

'Okay.' She kisses my forehead. Then she makes sure the door is locked and says, 'Come on,' and starts walking through the basement.

There's nothing in the basement. It's mostly just one huge room and it's pretty much empty. It's kinda damp cos the canal runs right beneath the windows. Outside, weeds crawl out of the stones and drag down the walls like the beard of a monster growing from the water.

Ma built us a toilet in one corner of the basement. It's an old plastic chair that she cut a hole into and then shoved a bucket beneath. When we use it, we just tip the bucket out the window into the canal. Ma says it makes no difference – it all ends up in the sea anyway.

The mill has six floors. Every floor has one huge room and one small room, with a staircase in between. The stairs run from the basement all the way up to the top, and the big rooms are all on the left and the small rooms are all on the right. Down here we call the small room the kitchen. It's not a real kitchen or anything. I think Ma just calls it that so she can pretend that the Castle is a real home.

There's only one window in the kitchen. Upstairs, right above the kitchen, is our bedroom and that has just one window too. Ma made us real beds by lifting our mattresses on top of crates. And we have real curtains, with pictures of boats on a sea. The sea used to be blue, and the boats were all different colours, but they're mostly faded now. We even have a shelf beside the window with loads of books on it. Much more than when we slept on the streets. I only had two then. But I lost them when the Authorities took Ma's rucksack, the same night they almost took me.

The best part of the bedroom is the duvet on my bed, cos it matches the curtains. I don't even care that they're all faded now. Cos a real room has curtains that slide, with a matching duvet cover. So when Ma brought them back, I knew we were here to stay.

She brought back a furry rug one day too, and now when I get out of bed it's like stepping onto fresh green grass.

The classroom is above the bedroom. That has my new school books, which are different from my bedtime books. They're for all different ages. Some are even for secondary school, like my science book, and Ma says I'm dead smart cos I understand them.

Ma goes through the basement, past the stairs and into the kitchen. I start to follow her.

I stop.

There's a shaft of light coming through a gap in one of the

boarded-up windows. It carries ripples inside from the canal like it's trying to tickle the floor. But it's real weird cos the air ripples too. I can see it, the air. It's full of dust, and the dust wobbles like it's being tickled too.

WHOOSH!

Something just flew through the dust! A shadow ran across the floor, I swear!

I stay dead still. Watch. Listen.

Nothing happens.

There's no shadow. The light on the floor doesn't ripple any more neither. I look around the room at all the shafts of light reaching through the gaps like the fingers of a giant feeling around for lost treasure. I keep waiting, but I don't see anything.

I turn and walk towards the kitchen pretending I don't care, but before I reach it I whip round to try and catch the shadow again. But it's not there now.

Maybe it's hiding in the dark corners. Or maybe whatever was there is gone. Cos the basement looks like it's asleep again.

I give up and go through the kitchen door.

There are pots and pans in one corner, stacked on some old shelves from the days when the mill was working. I think Ma got the pots in a charity shop at the same time that she bought a load of plates and bowls. Some of the plates are white and some are red and some have stripes. Right now, most of them are sitting in a big grey bucket that's on the ground in the corner, filled with brown water.

I can see Ma, through the kitchen window, standing in

the backyard. Beneath the window is the two-ring gas stove that Ma got for next to nothing in the same charity shop. But she didn't buy the table and the two chairs that are sitting in the middle of the room. She robbed those – I seen her do it.

There's a bakery next door and one day when no one was looking, she walked out the front door, round to the bakery and she picked up the table and chucked it over the gate into the backyard. Then she chucked the chairs in too. Then she ran off down the street and she hid for a while before she came back. But no one saw her. Ma's real good at nicking stuff.

I go through the kitchen and out the other door to join Ma in the backyard. I don't know what she's doing cos she's just standing there.

The Silo and the mill are side by side, with just a small gap between them. That's the backyard. Ma says 'silo' is just a fancy name for storage. It's where they used to store the grain that came down the canal and was going to get ground up in the mill. It looks like a massive grey cereal box. And it's twice as high as the mill. Maybe three times.

It's deadly cos the backyard is totally cut off from the city. On one end, the street where Ma was begging is blocked by a wall and a fat metal gate that never opens, and on the other end, the canal runs right past the Silo and the backyard and the mill, and then off under a bridge and through the city and into the river and then the sea.

We even have our own little beach, though you wouldn't go swimming in the canal cos it's full of rubbish and germs and you'd catch your death. There's no sand neither, but you can make brick castles instead of sandcastles from all the bricks lying around.

Across the canal from the beach there's this warehouse with no windows. So there's no way anyone could ever see us in the backyard. Unless maybe if they came past in a boat or something, but that almost never happens cos no one really uses the canal any more.

Ma looks up at the roof of the mill and I follow her gaze. I don't think she's looking at anything, though. I think she's listening.

The sun's moved over the canal now but I still have to squint. There are seagulls flying around the sky-bridge that joins the top of the mill to the side of the Silo, halfway up it.

I think the sky-bridge was there so the workers didn't have to plod all the way down the six floors of the mill and across the backyard to the Silo every time they wanted to grab a bag of grain. Instead they just crossed the bridge. There's a door up there that goes into the Silo. You can't get into it now, though, cos it's all locked up, but from the sky-bridge you can run up a ladder that's stuck to the side of the Silo, all the way to the roof, and from there you can see the whole city.

Ma's head snaps back down. She starts walking real fast over to the huge pile of crates and bricks that are stacked in the corner of the backyard against the gate and the wall.

'Ma?' I say. 'What are you doing?'

She runs up the crates and bricks, and sticks her head over so she can see into the skips on the other side.

'Ma?'

'Shh!' she says but she doesn't turn round.

Maybe she's heard the Authorities. Maybe they're climbing the wall to try to get to me. I take a step backwards. 'Ma?' I whisper.

But then Ma shouts over the wall, 'Here, what are yis doing with that?'

I hear voices reply but I don't know what they say.

'Chuck it over here, will ye?' Ma says to whoever is out there. And I don't think it's the Authorities cos she always uses her posh voice with the Yellow Jackets. She's scared of them too, but not as scared as I am. Cos they're after me, not her. 'Yeah, up here –' Ma is saying. 'Just chuck it over.' Ma turns to me. 'Come here a sec,' she says.

I don't move but she gives me her egg-sucking face and says, 'Come here and give me a hand!' so I run over. Something appears over my head on the wall. The bottom of it is brown and made of wood. It looks like some kind of furniture.

'That's grand,' Ma shouts over the wall and she grabs the wooden bottom and pulls on it. 'Keep going!'

I stand beneath it, step up on some bricks and crates, and just barely touch the corner with my fingertips. It starts tilting towards us.

'Yeah, keep going,' Ma yells.

'What is it, Ma?' I ask.

Someone must've been dumping it into the skip and Ma's gotten them to chuck it over the wall instead. But before I can figure out what it is, Ma loses her hold and it comes sliding over the wall and right for my head. I drop down onto the bricks but they start crumbling and tumbling under my feet. I shove my hands out but the thing ploughs into me. It's real heavy and it knocks me over and I'm falling backwards.

'Jaysus!' Ma says.

My leg's twisting – it's real sore! Now the thing's on top of me. I slip, and it slips, and I slide backwards, down the pile of crates and bricks, head first.

I think I'm upside down. There's a brick sticking into my ear. The wooden thing's on top of me. I wiggle and it wobbles like an elephant on a matchstick. Then there's a bit of light and Ma's face appears.

'Jaysus, love! Are ye all right?'

I think about this for a second. 'Yeah, I'm grand,' I say. I am. 'Hurt my elbow. And my leg a bit.'

'Ah, Jaysus. Sorry. Wasn't thinking,' Ma says. 'You're all right, though?'

'Here? Yis all right?' I hear a man yell.

'Are ye?' Ma asks and her face is all scrunched up.

'I'm grand, Ma,' I say.

'Sure?'

'Yeah.'

Ma smiles and the worry melts away.

'Yeah, we're grand, thanks,' Ma yells. Then her head

disappears and she shouts, 'Here, do yis have any more cushions with that?'

No one answers.

'What is it, Ma?'

Ma's face appears again. She grins. 'It's a couch. Do ye like it?'

'Eh, it's not very comfortable,' I say, and this makes Ma laugh so hard that I laugh too.

'Here, quit hogging the couch,' she says. 'Give us a go.' Ma starts chucking bricks aside and climbs in underneath.

'Ah, Ma, stop – it's going to go flying again!' I say. 'Get it off me!'

But Ma just says, 'Here, squidge over,' and she keeps squirming until she's upside down too and her face is right up next to mine. She pokes the couch with her finger. 'What do ye think?' I look at her and say nothing, so she goes on. 'Well, I like it.'

It's leather, I think. A two-seater. Brown. One of its arms is behind my head and I'm squished up against the cushions.

Ma pushes her hand against it and it moves.

'Careful, Ma!' I say.

'Good and firm. Not too worn. We'll get a blanket for it and it'll be good as new,' she says. 'I think we should keep it here and crawl in whenever it rains.'

'Or when the sun's too strong.'

''Zactly,' Ma says.

And even though there are pieces of brick poking my legs and my back and my bum, I don't care any more. 'I do think we should keep it outside, though,' I say.

'Yeah?'

'Yeah,' I say.

'What if it rains?' Ma says.

'We can shove that plastic sheet in the basement over it,' I say.

She turns her head so she's facing me. 'Good thinking, Batman!' she says. 'And I'll nick a table and chairs for outside too. And a barbecue. And I'll ask someone to build us a little sun deck. That'd be nice.'

I think of Rapunzel in her Castle. 'And a balcony too – off the bedroom. I'll grow my hair real long so it hangs all the way to the ground.'

'And your prince can climb up and rescue you.'

'Nah. I don't need a prince. Or rescuing. This is our Castle and we're staying.'

'Fair enough, you're the boss,' Ma says. Then she says, 'Sure you're all right?'

'Sure I'm sure,' I say.

Ma nods. 'Good,' she says. And she leans her forehead against mine till they touch and holds it there for a second. Then she says, 'Ready?' and she means, 'Let's go.'

'Yeah,' I say, and Ma starts to climb back out.

THE TOWER

Ma's lying on the couch with a wet towel draped over her face and her hair sprawled out over the side. After we dragged it to the middle of the backyard, Ma wiped it down and then stood there for ages looking at it and saying over and over, 'Not a thing wrong with that,' even though it's pretty ripped in places.

I'm watching her and thinking of the shadow in the basement. And the coins disappearing. But I can't do anything till Ma goes out. And I don't think she's going to move for a while.

I'm going up to the Silo roof to make sure the Authorities are definitely gone.

I tiptoe back through the kitchen and past the stairs, and then I run into the basement real quick to see if I can catch the shadow. I don't see anything, though. I'm not surprised. There are loads of pillars and corners in here. Plenty of ways for shadows to mix.

I turn back and run up the stairs, up, up, up, all the way to the sixth floor. At the top of the stairway, I sprint through a door and then I'm outside and I'm running across the sky-bridge. It goes right out over nothing, like running through the sky. It's got loads of holes but they're real small so you can't fall through. And way down below me is Ma lying on the couch with a towel over her face.

I get to the ladder, and climb up the Silo as fast as I can go, which is real fast cos I do it every day. When I get to the top, I run straight to the side where we were begging. I look down to the street. The Yellow Jackets are gone. I look left and right but I can't see them. Just people walking between the offices and apartment blocks and coffee shops.

I head for the other side of the roof, but there are no Yellow Jackets on the bridge neither. I look down the canal, along the streets and paths on the other side, till I can't hardly make out one building from another. Except for the spires of the churches and cathedrals. They're real easy to see.

The Authorities are gone. We're safe.

I lean against the wall and breathe out heavy. I didn't even realize I was holding my breath.

There are clouds coming in from the sea. They're piling up over the city but you can see the places where the sun gets through the holes in the clouds. The rays reach down through the sky and touch the buildings below, like the fingers of the giant in the basement, searching for the souls of dead people to take them up, out of this world.

The river cuts right through the city. It comes from the mountains. Usually you can see the mountains real clear, but today is so sunny that you can't hardly see them cos the air's all wavy.

That's where Ma says Care is. Out in the mountains. Care is the place where the Authorities take you. They lock you up and you can never see your ma again.

But it's where the enchanted forest is too. Cos enchanted forests are always in the mountains.

I like being up here. There's one church that's two streets away. It has a clock and a bell and a skinny steeple, and it strikes one dong for every quarter hour. Four dongs means it's a new hour. And at noon it just goes mental.

My favourite thing to do on the roof is snoop on people. There's this one woman that wears a red coat. Every morning, when the clock on the church is at around 8.40, I spot her way off down the streets. She's walking by the canal with this guy that's probably her husband or boyfriend. They look real funny cos she's tall and he's small. But they're always talking when they're walking, all the way up the canal. I don't think they ever run out of things to say to each other.

At around 8.50 they cross the bridge. When they reach this side of the canal I lose them cos the mill is in the way, but I know they come down off the bridge and walk along the street by our basement, right past the place where old man Caretaker sleeps.

Ma calls him Caretaker cos he always sleeps in the same spot, in a sheltered little area that's covered by a tin roof, between the outside wall of the mill and the street. Him being there all the time makes it seem like Caretaker's guarding the mill.

It doesn't even have four walls cos on the right the ground rises up slowly like a ramp till it reaches street level. It's where the carts used to drive down and load up, years and years ago, when the mill was still working.

There's a window in our basement that peeks into his shelter. It used to be boarded up but I pulled the top two boards away. On that side of the mill the basement is lower than the street so when you crouch on the ledge, all you can see of people above is their feet.

Sometimes I climb out and sit with him. It's not really outside, though, cos if I sit in the right place, people on the street above can't see me.

Caretaker's weird. He likes blankets and books and tins of sardines. And he never ever, washes. Ever.

After Red Coat and Short Guy have passed Caretaker, they get to the corner of the mill. That's where I see them again. They cross the road at the traffic lights and Short Guy kisses Red Coat. Then he walks straight on, towards the church, and I don't see him any more. But she turns and walks down the street beneath me and goes into one of the office buildings. I don't know where she goes after that cos she doesn't have a desk by a window.

But every day after 1.00 she comes out of the building and walks up the street and picks a coffee shop. She buys two coffees and two sandwiches and sits outside. On Fridays, she buys a muffin too.

26

Ten minutes later Short Guy turns up. He looks outside every coffee shop till he finds her. And when he does, he makes this face like he's so surprised she picked the one she did. And she laughs.

Every day she laughs.

And for the next forty minutes they talk between mouthfuls of sandwiches and coffee. And on Fridays, they share the muffin. But he only takes a little and then gives her the rest of his share.

I think he must have a real interesting job. Maybe he's the cleaner in the church and he snoops outside the confession box. Cos he always has a story to tell her and she always laughs.

At 1.55 they get up. He goes back towards the church and she goes back to her office. The next time I see her is after 5.00, when she leaves and walks down the road. She waits at the traffic lights till Short Guy arrives. And they kiss. Then they cross the street and walk right past the mill and Caretaker, then over the bridge and along by the canal, chatting, chatting, chatting, till the buildings and the traffic and the people swallow them up.

Sometimes they stop on the bridge and look down the canal. Sometimes they buy bread from a bakery and feed the swans. Sometimes they sit at a table outside a bar by the canal and drink wine. But never once in the last year and eight months have they stopped and looked up here. Never once have they noticed me. Or the mill. No one ever does.

Except for those men in the yellow jackets earlier. They noticed the mill.

It's weird cos I know I used to live down there, out on the streets, but even if I look all day, every day, I never see anything I recognize. But I remember it all. The alleyways and the doorways and the cans and the fighting and the shouting and the hiding and the hunger and the cold and the dark and the scary nights.

But it didn't start off like that. It used to be real good. Before it went real bad.

FEEDING THE FISHES

We've lived in loads of places. But Gran's was the best. Gran had a fireplace with a statue of the Virgin Mary with a little bowl of holy water on the mantelpiece, and when Gran and Ma would fight, Gran would dip her fingers in the bowl and say, 'Lord bless us and save us.'

Her house smelled of toast and soap and burning coal. I remember sitting beside Gran on the couch in our slippers, watching TV and eating eggs and rashers. And sometimes Gran would put rollers in her hair to curl it and she'd do mine too. But we'd take them out before we went to bed. And I wouldn't care what time Ma came home or how drunk she got, cos if I fell asleep in front of the fire, I'd wake up in bed with a load of blankets on me and it would be just as warm.

I had a plastic pink lunchbox with a handle, like a suitcase only much smaller. And Gran would put ham sandwiches in it for me and maybe an apple. Every school day she'd help me put on my navy school coat with the red symbol on the chest pocket. She'd say, 'Ready for work?' and then she'd hand me my lunchbox and we'd walk to school.

The school had a concrete yard as big as the Silo roof. In one corner was a garden with a pond. There were these tiny bubbles in the pond water that grew and grew till they became like marbles, except they weren't made of glass, they were made of jelly. And one day the bubbles were gone and instead there were hundreds and hundreds of black tadpoles swimming around in the pond, and that's when I learned that spawn becomes tadpoles and then they become frogs. And I thought that was deadly.

There was a girl called Claire and she liked the frog pond too. The teacher made us the Pond Monitors, which meant every day we had to stay back after school to check that no plastic had blown into it. We were the only ones allowed to sprinkle food for the fishes. They'd nibble the flakes and Claire would put her finger in the water, and the fishes thought her finger was food and nibbled it too. I did it as well but I couldn't stay still cos it tickled and made me laugh, and all the fishes got scared and hid.

Gran would meet me and Claire at the gates of the school and walk us home. If it was hot she'd buy ice cream. One for Claire too, even though she wasn't her gran. If it was winter we'd all share a bag of chips or something.

We passed Claire's house first. Gran and her ma would always end up drinking tea and talking for ages, so we'd go play with her toys. Claire had a room all to herself with a box filled with dolls and she'd let me play with them. Except if they were her favourites. I wasn't allowed to touch those.

At Easter she got a mountain of chocolate eggs. She wouldn't eat them, though. She just left them stacked there. She didn't even open them.

I got two. One from Gran and one from Ma. But they were really both from Gran cos I'd seen them in a bag under her bed when I went snooping in her room. I'd eaten them both by lunchtime on Easter Sunday but Claire still had all hers when school finished for summer.

I don't know if she ever ate them cos Ma and Gran had a massive fight after that and we left.

It was just after the first night of the summer holidays. Me and Gran were sitting out on the porch with curlers in our hair, doing a jigsaw puzzle of the ocean.

I was trying to finish a dolphin when Ma came out the front door with her bag and coat. She kissed my forehead.

'Where are ye going, all dolled up?' Gran said. It was weird cos I thought Ma looked great, but Gran said it like it was a bad thing.

'Out,' Ma said, and opened the little front gate that didn't close properly.

Gran said something about Ma winning a prize.

I looked up then. 'What did you win, Ma?'

I'd won first prize for drawing in school. The teacher gave me a brand new paint set.

But Ma said, 'Me? Nothing. Gran's winning the Best Mother prize these days, aren't you, Gran?'

Ma let go of the gate and came back. She found the next piece of the dolphin and put it in the right place. Then she said, 'Funny, don't remember doing a lot of jigsaws meself when I was a kid.'

'Don't start with that,' Gran said.

'Don't remember doing a lot of anything,' Ma said. 'There's some stuff I remember only too well, though.'

I thought that maybe Ma was upset cos she didn't have a jigsaw. 'You can have this one, Ma. There are three pieces missing. But it still works.'

Ma smiled then, and leaned down till her forehead was touching mine. 'I'll be back later, love,' she whispered.

Then she started walking away. But when she got to the path she shouted over her shoulder, 'Have fun, girls. Remember, it's never too late to make up for lost time. Ha, *Gran*?' And she said Gran like it was a joke name or something. I looked at Gran to see if she was laughing. She wasn't. She was watching Ma walk down the street.

'We cooked yet?' I said.

Gran turned to me with a funny look. Her face could change real quick, just like Ma's. Sometimes it was as sharp as a witch's. It didn't scare me, though.

'What are you talking about?' she asked.

I pointed to the curlers in my hair.

Gran laughed then and her face went all soft and wrinkly, like an old mushroom. 'Nearly. Finish the jigsaw first.'

*

That night when Gran put me to bed, Ma wasn't home. But in the morning when I woke, she was already up and packing a bag.

'Get up,' Ma said. 'We're going on holidays.'

'Ah, Ma,' I said. I didn't want to. I'd gone on holidays with Ma before. It usually meant staying in some poxy flat with one of her mates.

But Ma had packed a rucksack and she was going. And once Ma's going, no one can stop her. Not even Gran.

She tried anyway, though. She stood in Ma's way when she was dragging me out the door. But Ma just shoved her aside.

Gran was shouting. She said, 'For God's sake, act like a mother!'

But Ma already had me out the front door. 'Coming from you of all people?' she said. 'That's bleeding rich!'

'Ah, Jaysus, how many times can I say sorry?' Gran said.

'Not enough,' Ma said. 'Not enough.'

Ma tried to slam the gate shut but it wouldn't close.

'At least tell me where yis are going,' Gran said.

'To the beach!' Ma said. She kicked the gate and started storming up the road.

I kept looking back at Gran as Ma dragged me away. She was standing there in the doorway. I'd seen Ma and Gran fight before. But this was different. Cos Gran didn't look witchy this time. She looked like she'd been walking all day and just realized she was back where she'd started.

That's when things started to go bad.

CURRY CHIPS AND
A BATTERED SAUSAGE

It's getting late and I still need Ma to go out so I can nick some coins and make sure there's nothing scary lurking in the mill. I turn round and run across the roof and climb down the ladder and run across the sky-bridge and into the mill and down the stairs and through the kitchen.

'Ma,' I say when I get to the door. She's still lying on the couch. 'I'm hungry.'

I startle a cat that's been sniffing around. It leaps away and scurries up the bricks and crates. It looks dead scabby, half its fur missing. When it gets to the wall it sits there staring at me like it thinks I'm going to eat it or something. There are two more cats on the wall. Little ones. They stare at me too. Cats don't like me. They don't seem bothered by Ma, probably cos she always feeds them. But they run when I come out.

'Ma,' I say again when she doesn't answer. 'I'm hungry.'

'Have some bread,' Ma says, but with the towel on her face it sounds like 'Hasobre'.

'I don't want bread,' I say.

The bakery next door uses one of the skips. They throw out enough food to feed half the city. The other one is used by everyone and you can find loads of deadly stuff in it, like books and rusted bikes and wooden chairs and old mattresses. Or couches.

Every day we fish out sandwiches and scones from the bakery's skip, and even fruit that has nothing wrong with it, except it's gone a little black or has a dent in it or something.

But I don't want fruit.

'I want chips,' I say, cos that means Ma will have to go out.

'Just let me relax for ten bleeding minutes, will ye?' she says, which is stupid cos she's been lying there for ages sunbathing. 'You can't be hungry again.'

Some gulls screech and I look up and see them swooping down this way from the sky-bridge. The bakery probably just threw out some bread and they've seen it.

'Fine, I'll go get the chips,' I say.

'Dream on,' she says. 'You'll stay here.'

Of course I will. But I offered cos it always works.

I can't go outside. If I'm seen, it's game over. Sitting on the top step by the front door or in Caretaker's room or by our beach is as far as I can go. But that's fine with me. I don't want to go out there anyway.

Ma sighs and gets up but then grabs the side of the couch and just hovers there.

36

'Jaysus, lying down too long,' she says. 'Made me all dizzy.'

She shakes the dizziness away and stands. She stares down at herself. I really wish she'd hurry up but she says, 'Look at the state of me,' and goes over to the tap by the wall and fills the bucket and dips a bar of soap into it and then scrubs her face and arms. She leans over, lifts the water up, and pours it over her head and yelps as it sploshes all over.

I try to stay still cos when I get impatient, like I am now, I always tap my foot or bite my nails and it's a dead giveaway that I'm up to something Ma wouldn't like.

'Jaysus, that's freezing,' she says, like she says every time. Her hair's dripping and hangs like slimy eels over her shoulders. It's soaking her T-shirt but she doesn't care. 'So, what do ye want?'

'Curry chips and a battered sausage,' I say, like I always say. 'And Coke.'

'Is that all?' she asks, real sarcastic.

'And a surprise.'

'A surprise, me granny,' she says and she picks up the cup and I really, really hope she doesn't take all the coins. But she tips the money into her hand, picks out the bigger ones and throws the copper coins back. I can relax now cos there are loads of coins left.

'Don't forget the batteries,' I say.

She nods. 'What are you going to do?'

'Read,' I lie, and she gives me a look.

'Don't even think of going anywhere, ye hear me? You go

out there and I'll lose ye and never be able to find ye,' she says. 'What'll I do if I find out you've gone out there?'

'You'll knock me sideways,' I say.

'Bloody sure!' she says.

I don't say anything to her as we pass through the empty basement cos I'm dying for her to leave now, but it's pretty dark in here and Ma trips over my bike and she almost falls but stops herself just in time.

'I told ye not to leave that thing lying around. I'll break my bleeding neck one of these days!'

'Sorry, Ma!' I say and I pick it up and wheel it to a wall and follow her to the door.

She's still rubbing her shin. 'Jaysus, that hurts,' she says. She bends down and kisses me. 'I'll be back soon, promise. Don't forget to lock this door,' she says, like always.

She goes out onto the street and I take the key off the hook by the door and lock it from the inside. Then I run through the basement to the side where Caretaker lives. I creep up to the window, climb up on the ledge and peek out. I can't see Caretaker cos he's hidden by a pile of blankets. But after a minute I see Ma's feet arrive above him.

'Heya,' I hear Ma say to Caretaker.

'Howaye,' he says in a voice like a truck reversing over gravel.

'I'm heading out. Need anything?'

'Nope. Took a stroll around earlier, I did. All sorted. But thank you kindly,' he says.

Then the traffic picks up and I can't hear what Ma says.

I try to listen real hard, cos I want to know if they're going to talk about the Authorities turning up outside the Castle. But the only thing I hear is Caretaker saying stuff like 'planning permission' and 'Silicon Docks' and 'starting in January', which is real boring and doesn't have anything to do with me.

I get up and run to the backyard. I have more important things to do than snoop on boring conversations.

A TRAIL OF BREADCRUMBS

I'm back in the basement but this time my pockets jingle with change. It's damp in here and my arms go all goosebumpy. Even though it's sunny outside, in the shade it's cold. Tomorrow is October. In a few weeks it'll be winter and this place will be like a fridge.

There's not a lot in here from the old days – just six arches that run across the room from one side to the other and loads of pipes on the ceiling.

Most of my stuff is in the basement, like my bike and my rollerblades. I even made a basketball net by cutting a hole out of a bucket and tying it to the ceiling. This is the best room for practising basketball cos it has a concrete floor. But I don't want to practise right now.

I crouch behind the pillar of the middle arch and listen. Outside, the city is moving and growing, but in here there's no sound. I watch the shafts of light in the air. The dust just hangs there not moving, not even a little bit.

Ma says bottles and plastic bags and clothes and tree branches float down the canal cos they're lighter than water, and I wonder if that means dust is the same weight as air if it floats in it, cos if it was lighter than air, it would float to the ceiling and if it was heavier, it would be on the floor. But then that doesn't make sense cos there's loads of dust on the floor too – I can see our footprints in it.

But I remember why I'm here and I take a coin from my pocket and put it right in the middle of one of the fingers of light on the floor.

Then I go to the next space between the arches and do the same. And the next. And then I run back towards the stairs and the kitchen, dropping coins between the last two arches till there are five coins on the ground in total.

Now I need to do the same on the next floor, so I run up the stairs. I ignore our bedroom and go straight into the big room on the left.

This floor is different. It has arches too, but the pillars aren't so wide. And there's old machines that are real rusted and lying on their sides like they've been stabbed and keeled over and died. There are loads of pipes up here as well. Much more than in the basement. They run higgledy-piggledy all over the ceiling and down the walls.

I leg it around the room putting coins on top of the dead machinery. Five in total.

Then it's up to the next floor where the classroom is. But

I don't go into it. I just close the door and go back across the stairway into the big room on this floor.

I like the third floor. There are weird-looking tubes in it. Some are fat and reach from the floor up to the ceiling. Others are like mouths with lids, and you can open them and stick your head in and make noises that flow down to the next floor and roll through it and climb the stairs and echo back through this room again.

I put a coin on each lid and then run back to the stairs and up to the fourth floor, where the boards are all rotted and if you fall through, you'll break your neck. But I know which boards creak and which ones are broken and which ones are strong.

I stay close to the wall. In the middle of the room there's a pipe sticking right up in the air, like the picture of a periscope on a submarine that I saw in a book. Hardly any of the windows are boarded up in here and there are a thousand little suns like spiders' eyes reflecting off the pipes.

I have to crawl across a pipe cos the ground beneath it is rotted. When I get to the periscope, I climb down and crouch on the floor. I put one ear to the open pipe and cover my other ear, and the world goes all fuzzy, like when I'm standing on the roof in the wind.

I listen. After a while my neck starts to cramp cos I'm leaning over, and my legs start to hurt, but I don't move an inch. I just squeeze my eyes closed and concentrate real hard. But after ages I still don't hear anything.

I open my eyes. I don't move. The thousand suns are gone.

I look outside. 'Red sky at night, shepherd's delight,' I whisper and it's so still that I imagine the words are just drifting in the air with the dust.

Then I hear the sound. It's like when you're turning a page but it's stuck to the next one and you lick your fingers and rub the pages and eventually they come apart.

I lift my head and stare at the mouth of the pipe. I hear it again, the weird shuffling sound, and I put my ear tight against the periscope and cover my other ear and listen real hard.

Shuffle, shuffle, shuffle, stop.

It's coming from one of the floors below. It sounds like a dead person dragging its mangled body across the ground.

Shuffle, shuffle, shuffle, stop.

Then silence. There's nothing. I sit up.

Thump, thump, thump.

That sound's not coming from the pipe. It's coming from the stairs. Something is climbing the stairs!

Thump, thump, thump.

It's getting closer. I don't know what to do. The door is ages away, I'll never make it out of here in time.

Thump, thump, thump.

I can hear a jingling noise too. It must be the coins. I make a little scared sound, which is real stupid.

It stops. There's no more thumping. I wait. I put my ear back to the pipe and I hear more shuffling. It's on one of the other floors.

Shuffle, shuffle, shuffle, stop.

44

I want to run. I want to go up onto the roof. But I can't. I have to stay and listen. Cos this is my home and I'm never leaving here. So I have to find out.

It's moving around. I hear it. Starting and stopping and starting again. A hundred times I think I'm going to run away but a hundred times I decide to stay and listen.

Then it stops. I lift my head. Try to hear if the *shuffle, shuffle, shuffle* turns into *thump, thump, thump*. I hold my breath. Nothing happens.

Ages and ages passes. Maybe it's gone? I wait longer.

The sky's not orange any more and the room's bluey-grey and the pipes melt into the ceiling. I still don't hear anything. I think it's gone.

I crawl over the pipe and step onto the floor by the wall. I creep real slow over the boards, cos I can't see which are broken now that it's dark. I get to the door and look down the stairs and listen. Only the sounds of the city outside, clanking and humming and beeping.

I go down. Step by step. Real soft. My heart's going mental – *thump, thump, thump* – hammering in my ears. At the third floor, I crouch down and wait. But I don't hear anything else.

I take a massive breath and I run downstairs to our bedroom. I nearly trip on Ma's clothes on the floor cos I can't hardly see. I grab my torch. No batteries. I fling all Ma's clothes off the bed till I find her torch by her pillow. I click it on and the beam blinds me. I hold the light against my stomach and run on my tippy-toes back up the stairs and onto the third floor.

45

It's quiet. I take a deep breath and I swing the torch around. I can see the lids of the tubes and the floorboards and a broken pipe. I shine it over the whole room. Stop on one of the lids.

There's no coin.

My legs are shaky but I have to look. I force myself to walk through the room.

It's the same at every lid. No coin.

I creep back down to the next floor. I go from fallen machine to fallen machine but no matter where I look, the coins are gone, gone, gone.

I don't even need to look in the basement, but I do. I run straight across it, pointing the torch on the ground. I don't see a single coin and I don't stop. I go to the front door and I rattle it but it's definitely still locked. It's only me in the Castle.

And now I know, a hundred thousand per cent, that the mill is haunted.

I turn and shine the torch through the dust. The dust is moving! The ghost is still here! I jump backwards and knock into the door. I take a deep breath. Hold it.

The dust stops moving when I stop breathing.

It's not the ghost, it's just me.

Behind me the door rattles. I spin round.

I stare at it. I step away. It's silent now. Nothing. Maybe I made it up. Maybe it didn't rattle.

Suddenly the door trembles and the whole basement booms.

Knock, knock . . . knock.

I can't move.

Knock, knock . . . knock.

It's right outside the door.

But then I hear coughing and I know that cough. It's Ma.

I grab the key and shove it in the keyhole. I yank the door so fast that it hits me in the face. Ma steps in and the smell of salt and vinegar expands in the room.

'Jaysus, what's up with you?' Ma says.

I stare at her.

'Ye all right?' she says.

'Yeah,' I whisper.

She holds up two bags. She nods her head at one – 'Food.' Then the other – 'Batteries for the lights.'

I nod, that's all. What am I supposed to say, 'Ma, the Castle is haunted'? I've a feeling 'haunted' would be a new Stress Word.

'Speaking of lights . . .' Ma clicks a switch by the door and a trail of stars like the Milky Way appears above us, running through the basement to the kitchen. 'At least those batteries are still working. Better change the ones in the kitchen, though.' She means the fairy lights we put up after we found them in the skip last Christmas.

'And remind me to put them in your torch too.' Ma pushes past me. 'Come on, I'm starving,' she says. 'Hurry up or I'll eat yours too.'

CASTLES IN THE SAND

After we left Gran's, Ma got us a tent from somewhere and for a while we lived down in the dunes on the other side of the harbour wall where the big ships come in from the sea, carrying containers stacked like Lego. Ma laughed at me when I called them dunes. She said, 'You've some imagination, love.'

But they were made of sand, and there were hills and holes where you could hide and no one else could see you. And there were even these green plants, like long grass, growing out of them. So Ma was wrong. They *were* dunes. Even if they weren't big yellow ones like you see in books.

When you were in the tent at night and the flap was open, you couldn't see much, just the sand dune in front of you. But you could hear the sound of the sea and you could pretend you were way up in the mountains and the

49

sound was the wind flowing through an enchanted forest and there was no one else around for miles and miles.

When the tide went out, the beach stretched to the end of the world. It was full of broken shells and glass and plastic. One day, when it was real sunny, Ma was lying on a towel relaxing and I was digging a hole beside her. A little further down the beach there was a boy making sandcastles.

They were real good cos he had a big red bucket and a small yellow bucket, and when he filled the red one up with sand and turned it upside down, it made round castles with little squares on top.

He was using the buckets to make one massive sandcastle. It was more like a city than a castle, though. It had loads of floors and each of them had towers on them. And it had a big space in the middle with some towers in that too.

I watched him for ages and then I went over to him and said, 'Here, can I have a go of your bucket?'

He looked at me and then he looked over to his ma, who was sitting on one of those folding chairs near the dunes, so I said real quick, 'I won't nick it or anything. I just want to have a go.'

He didn't answer but he threw the red bucket at my feet and watched me. I shoved handfuls of sand into it and turned it over to make a castle. It didn't stand up like his did, though. It just crumbled back into sand. But he showed me how to pack the sand real tight so that when you turned the bucket over, the castle didn't fall apart. Then he even let me help him build his.

He was making a big wall around the whole thing and he told me to dig a moat to protect the castle. The only way to cross it was over the drawbridge and you could pull it up at a second's notice.

I found a knot of wood for the drawbridge. Flat shells are real good for windows. And labels off plastic bottles for flags.

I ran up past Ma and grabbed a load of dune grass. Then I cut it up real small to make a garden inside the castle. The castle even had cannons to fight off the pirates. I made them from shells that looked like tubes and I stuck them into the walls. It was the best sandcastle I'd ever seen.

In the middle of working on it, his ma brought over sandwiches. They were filled with cheese but they had some sand stuck in them too. She had apples and yogurts and cartons of orange juice as well and she just gave me one of everything, the same as him.

My ma saw us all there and she came over with biscuits and crisps. She started chatting to his ma about real boring stuff like the weather. But it was grand cos if Ma was talking about the weather, it meant she hadn't been drinking. And her hands hadn't started to shake that much back then neither, so she looked dead normal.

I looked up at our tent but you couldn't see it cos it was behind a dune. And me and Ma were in our swimming togs, so we looked like everyone else. His ma probably didn't even know we were sleeping there. And I was happy cos I didn't want her to know.

Then our mas went back to their towels, but not before

my ma winked at me. After we ate, we kept working on the castle till it started to get cold. Then his ma said they had to go home and he turned and ran away. He didn't even care that he was leaving behind the best castle ever.

Ma came over then and sat with me. 'That's some castle,' she said. She flung her hair out behind her and she leaned back on her elbows. 'Ah yeah, I could get used to this.' She watched the sea for a while. 'If you could live anywhere in the world, where would it be?' she asked. But I didn't answer cos I didn't know anywhere else. Ma said, 'Greece. Or Portugal. Somewhere in the sun. No stress. Just white sand and blue sea. You could sit there and watch the sunset, sipping a sangria, with no one to annoy ye.' Ma started rubbing my back. 'Just you and me.'

I said, 'Kinda like here, now?'

And Ma laughed like I'd made a joke. But she didn't answer. Instead she said, 'What about you?'

'I'd live in a castle with seventeen rooms and loads of towers and a massive garden and a secret escape route.'

'Fair enough,' she said. 'Would there be room for me?'

''Course,' I said. 'There'd be loads of room. You'd have your own bedroom and everything.' Ma arched her eyebrows at me, so I said, 'But you could still share mine on nights you got scared.'

'Thanks, love,' she said and she pulled me down so I was lying beside her. Then we just lay there and I would have stayed all night but the sea came back in.

It was stupid but I remember thinking if I sat beside the

castle, the sea wouldn't come up that far. But it did. It kept coming. And even cannons can't stop the sea.

First, the moat filled up with water. Then the next wave made all the walls rounded. It carried the drawbridge out too. Each wave dissolved a little bit more of the castle, and it got smoother and flatter till the whole thing got washed away and it looked like the castle was never there. And there was nothing I could do but watch.

That's when Monkey Man and his mates turned up. But I didn't know how bad he was cos I'd never seen him before. If I'd known, I'd have made Ma leave straight away.

THE WITCH AND THE ALTAR

'What are you doing?'

I blink and look up at Ma. It's the second of October. My birthday. And two whole days since I found out that the Castle is haunted.

We're in the classroom. The walls are so crumbled they look like they have chickenpox. I've tried to cover the holes with pictures of castles and forests and drawbridges, but there are more holes than pictures on the walls.

Right now I'm supposed to be learning poxy maths but I can't concentrate. It's no wonder. Who can concentrate when they know that their house is haunted by a ghost that drags its mangled body around?

Ma taps my notebook with her fingernail. 'Finish this up and then we'll see about this birthday of yours.'

Maybe all castles are haunted. I think the real problem is knowing if it's a good ghost or a bad ghost.

'Here, you, concentrate!' Ma says.

I look at Ma. I don't think I should tell her about the ghost. 'Ah, Ma, it's my birthday, can't I have the day off?'

'No one gets a day off just cos it's their birthday,' Ma says. She leans back in her chair, which is a black one with a lever on the side so you can change the height. Ma found it on the side of the road when she was bargain hunting. She was real proud of herself when she dragged it through the front door one day. Lucky it had wheels cos it was so heavy it took both of us to carry it up the stairs. Then Ma stood there for ages looking at it and saying, 'Not a thing wrong with that,' over and over.

Ma sighs and I know she wants to be outside, not teaching me. She can't concentrate neither. She looks out the window like she's staring at the ocean and not at the wall of the Silo. Then she does this shiver thing where she shakes her shoulders and goes, 'Brrr! Someone just walked over me grave.'

She does that sometimes and I don't know what she means. 'Ma? I think there's a ghost in the mill,' I say, and I'm surprised cos I didn't think I was going to tell her.

Ma drags her eyes away from the window. 'What?'

I try to look at her but I'm too embarrassed, cos now I've said it out loud I know how stupid it sounds, so I stare down at my copy book instead. 'I heard something yesterday when you were out. Something was shuffling around and walking up the stairs and it . . .' I stop cos I don't want to tell her about the coins. I don't know why, I just don't want her to know, so instead I say, 'And it sounded like a ghost dragging its mangled body around.'

I look at Ma now, even though I'm real embarrassed that I told her that I think there's a ghost. I want to see if she laughs or if she believes me. But I can't tell.

She lifts her foot up onto the chair and rests her chin on her knee. After a while she says, 'A ghost? Hmm. You know, when I was a young one, around your age, there was this old church at the back of our street.'

I picture the church I can see from the roof with the skinny steeple and the big clock that dongs every fifteen minutes.

'It wasn't used any more,' she says. 'It was locked up and there was this ivy that had grown all over it.'

Now I'm picturing ivy creeping up the walls of the church, sneaking through the windows and crawling up the steeple till it's completely covered and you can't hardly see the clock any more. 'Like an octopus with long fingers,' I say.

Ma turns her head towards me so her cheek is resting on her knees. She looks at me for a minute. She's trying to figure out what I mean. When she cops on, she says, 'Tentacles, an octopus has tentacles. And yeah, it was kinda like a massive green octopus eating the church.'

I stay quiet so that she'll go on with the story.

'It was real scary-looking, that church,' she says. 'But the scariest part?'

'What?'

'A witch lived there.'

'Ah, Ma!' I say, and I throw my eyes up to the ceiling.

'What?'

'A witch?'

'Yeah,' she says. 'Are you listening or not?'

'Sorry,' I say.

'Right. Well, they said the witch used to sleep on the altar at night, lying there, stiff as a corpse. We were all real scared of that church and that witch. Still didn't stop me and me mates from messing with it every chance we got, though.'

I can't imagine Ma being my age. And I never liked any of Ma's mates.

'We used to bury eggs in the park beneath this big tree. We'd wait till they were rotten and real stinky. Then we'd dig them up and go over there to the church and open that creaky gate and stand on the path and throw the rotten eggs at the front of the church.' Ma sits up straight now. 'Jaysus, they stank.'

'Like what?' I ask.

'Like your farts on a bad day, that's like what.'

I laugh and Ma nods like she's dead serious.

'Anyway, this day we were all standing there on the path and we decided that one of us had to go in there and smash an egg right on top of the altar.'

'What, inside the church?'

'Yeah.'

I imagine the smell of farts filling up the church. 'Ugh.'

'Damn right! I'm the one who drew the short straw. Had to go in there all on me own.'

'How did you get in if it was all locked up?'

'I was a skinny yoke back then,' Ma says, as if she's not still mad skinny. 'A few of the windows had fallen in and I could squeeze through the iron bars. So that's what I did. Then one of me mates handed the rotten eggs in through the bars and they all stood there to watch me.'

Ma pauses for dramatic effect. All good stories need dramatic effect. I wait cos that's what I'm supposed to do.

'So there I am, creeping up that aisle towards the altar. Never been so scared in me whole life. It was weird in there. Dead still. I get about halfway up and I stop. Decide to chuck them from there. Lift me arm over me head –' Ma lifts her arm – 'and was about to throw one when suddenly, from the door behind the altar, she came flying out at me!'

'Who, the witch?'

'Yep.'

'Jaysus – what did she look like?'

'All I could see was flapping black rags and mad hair racing towards me. And, Jaysus, was she shrieking. I'm just standing there like an eejit. Mouth hanging open. I drop the eggs on the floor and they smash everywhere and they smell worse than hell.

'She comes roaring around the altar and down the steps. Me mates are there at the window behind me, screaming at me to move, and finally I snap out of it and I turn to run but I slip on the broken eggs. *Slap!*' Ma claps her hands and I jump in my seat. 'Straight down, face first into those rotten eggs. Well, between the smell and the fear, I puked, right there in the aisle, on top of the eggs.'

'Gross,' I say.

'Bleeding right. I've got puke and rotten egg all over me, and me mates are still screaming at me, and she's right behind me, so I jump up and run. But I've lost me shoe! Slipped off me foot when I fell.

'So I'm sprinting down the aisle with only one shoe and as soon as I get to the window, me mates are grabbing me and pulling me through, but I turn for a second and I see her. Grey face, grey eyes. Snarling at me, she was. Then I see her fingernails. They were real long, like claws, and she has my shoe in her hand. And you know what?'

I sit up straight and say, real proud of myself, 'She comes up and hands it to you!'

I know what Ma's doing. She's telling me a Moral. There's always a Moral to Ma's stories. And the Moral is that she wasn't a witch, she was a nice old woman. I'd bet the winning lotto ticket on it, if I had it.

Ma shakes her head. 'Nah. She chucks it right at me and hits me in the face.'

'Oh.'

'No word of a lie,' Ma says. 'Then I'm outside and we're all pegging it for the gate. Scariest day of me life.' Ma sits back and nods at me. 'I was battered for losing that shoe.'

I wait.

'Ma?' I say. 'What's the Moral?'

Ma crosses her arms behind her head and leans back. 'Don't break into a witch's house.'

'Ah, Ma, that's not the Moral, she probably wasn't even a witch!'

60

'Why?' she says.

'I don't know. Witches boil kids' bones or something. They don't just throw shoes.'

'Yeah? What would you do if someone broke in here and threw rotten eggs at ye?'

'I'd bleeding batter them,' I say.

"Zactly.' Ma's still leaning back with her arms behind her head. But there's a joke in her eyes and I know that I was right. I know there's a Moral coming. 'She was probably just as scared as me,' she says. 'Worse, cos it was her home. She felt safe there. Or expected to. And I broke in and tried to throw rotten eggs at her. 'Course she was mad. Mad as hell.'

'So she wasn't a witch,' I say, and I'm nodding cos I knew that all along.

'No. Just some weird, lonely auld one.'

I think about it. Ma's right. I'd hate it if someone broke into our Castle.

'But what about the ghost?' I say.

She laughs. 'Look, she thought I was a robber or a murderer or something, yeah? And I thought she was a witch. Neither of those things were true. We just made them up cos we were afraid. I mean, in the end, we were exactly what we were supposed to be. A stupid girl and a scared old woman. That's all.'

'So . . .' I say, and I'm saying it real slow cos I'm trying to figure out what Ma's point is. 'So when you're scared, you make things up?' And I know what she means. She means I didn't hear a ghost, I just thought I did. She doesn't know about the coins, though. 'But . . .' I say. That's all I say though cos I still don't want to tell her.

'But nothing,' she says. 'Just a stupid bleeding pigeon stuck in one of the rooms, that was all.' Ma says it real gentle, though. And she smiles. And she nods. And she lifts my hand and she kisses the top of each finger, one by one, like she used to do when we were on the streets and I was scared.

'Now, can we please get on with maths?' Ma is pushing my book in front of me again.

'Ah, Ma, come on, please? It's my birthday. Can't we finish early, just for today? This isn't even a real school, Ma.'

She looks at me. 'And you're better off for it. Real school is poxy.'

I think of arguing but she's already giving me her egg-sucking face. I decide on a different tactic. Bargain.

'Tell you what, Ma,' I say. 'I'll finish this whole page of sums – every single one of them – and I won't look up till I've finished and I won't say anything unless I need help. And when I'm finished, I'll take a science book outside with me and I'll read it while you sit in the sun.' I shove my head into my book till my nose is almost hitting the page and I don't look up again.

I hear her sigh and I know that sigh. It means I've won.

THE BIRTHDAY PRESENT

I finally finished all my sums and now we're in the backyard. I'm building a brick castle. It's massive. So big that I can crawl into it. I used bricks to build the walls and I put a crate on top for the roof. It's not enough, though. I need it to be waterproof in case it rains.

There's an island of rubbish floating down the canal. I bet there's loads of good stuff in it, but it's too far away to reach. There's something closer, though. It's white and square, like a big piece of paper. It's caught just past the corner of the mill.

I grab the stick we use for fishing stuff out of the canal, which is the same one we use for fishing food out of the skip. It's standing beside the door to the kitchen.

I kneel on our beach and lean out and catch it. Drag it in. It's plastic and hard. I grab it by the corner and pick it up. It's one of those posters they stuck up on all the lamp posts last month. It has a picture of a baldy man with a fake smile. It says,

VOTE KELLY
NO. 1
FOR REAL CHANGE

It's perfect. I slide it in between the gaps in the crate. Now all I need is a few more and my roof will be waterproof.

I watch the canal. I don't see another one anywhere. But I bet one will float by in the next few days.

I turn and look at Ma. She's on the couch reading an old newspaper. There's a half-eaten birthday cake on the table in front of her.

I wonder if I should tell her about the ghost coins. But maybe I'm being silly. Maybe it's not really a ghost. Something took those coins, though. Which means I have to investigate again. But this time, I'll stay on the second floor, not hide on the fourth. That way I'll be sure I see it and not just hear it.

Ma must feel me watching her cos she looks up and smiles. Then she looks past me. 'What's that?' she says, pointing to the canal. Something else is floating along.

I try to catch it but it's pretty far out.

'Careful,' Ma says, and I know she means 'Don't fall in', but she also means 'Don't let anyone see you'. Usually no one can see me cos straight across the canal from the backyard are just warehouses. But when I lean right out, people in offices or crossing the bridge could see me.

Ma comes over and helps me and right then the wind changes and whatever it is floats towards us and we have it.

Ma squeezes out the canal water. 'It's a hoody,' she says, and she stretches out the arms. 'And a bloody good one too.' She holds it up against me and I stand tall and roll my shoulders back. 'Like it was made for you.' She grins like she's just won the lotto and then goes to the tap and fills the bucket and starts washing it.

The way she scrubs it, you'd swear she'd rub a hole straight through it, and when she's done, she twists it as tight as a rope and hangs it on the line beside a blanket that's been there since morning and is probably bone dry by now. Then she takes a step back and puts her hands on her hips and says, 'Not a thing wrong with it.'

Ma turns to me. 'Happy birthday, love. Which reminds me . . .' She disappears inside and when she comes back, she's holding a plastic bag and she hands it to me.

Inside the bag is a box and I recognize it. It was in the skip weeks ago but when I went to fish it out, it was gone. Ma must have gotten to it before me and was hiding it all this time.

'What is it, Ma?' I ask, but she doesn't say so I open the box. 'Binoculars!'

Ma smiles and nods.

They're amazing. Real old. The strap is all hairy and the plastic's cracked. I bet they used to belong to an explorer. They've probably been all over the world.

I hold them up and I lean out and look over the canal at

the offices there. 'It's all blurry,' I say, but she shows me how to move the wheel and then I can see everything!

'Hey Ma, there's a man typing and I can see a cup beside him and it has writing on it that says "I love . . ." something. Spreadsheets! It says "I love spreadsheets". What's a spreadsheet?' Ma doesn't answer and I don't really care. I lean further. 'Ma! I can see the boys jumping off the bridge. This is deadly!'

They're wearing wetsuits and they have runners on. There are always boys jumping off the bridges and the buildings into the canal on sunny days. I don't think they care about all the rubbish in the water. Maybe their wetsuits protect them from catching their death.

I don't think they're allowed to be jumping cos sometimes the Authorities arrive in their yellow jackets. I've seen them. When they turn up, I always duck in case they see me. But the boys are real brave. They just shout at the Yellow Jackets and swim to the other side of the canal and run away before the Authorities can get them. Maybe it's cos there are loads of boys and they know that together they could fight the Authorities away.

There's only one of me, though, and I'm dead small.

One of the boys who is standing on the bridge pushes another who is standing on the railing and he goes flying forwards into the water, and the others are all shouting and laughing. I see him hit the water but it's a second before I hear the *splash!* and I laugh too.

I can even read the word 'Reebok' on the side of one of their runners and I realize something.

'Hey, Ma, now I'll be able to see right across the city and I might find Gran's house and my old school! And maybe we can move back there when I'm grown and the Authorities aren't after me any more!' And I turn to show her that I think this is the best present ever but the look on her face stops me dead.

It's her eyes. They're sinking. The way they used to when she got sad.

What did I do that for? Why did I mention Gran's house and the Authorities?

'Don't worry, Ma. The Authorities don't know I'm here. And with the binoculars, I can watch out for them coming. I'll see them a mile off. So we'll be able to prepare. I'll be like a soldier, guarding the Castle. They'll never get as close as they did in the alleyway that night.'

It's out before I can even think of what I'm saying. She stares at me like I'm on fire or something.

'It's grand, Ma. They didn't get me! You got back in the nick of time, remember?'

Ma's eyes sink even deeper. I need to shut up.

'You shouldn't be here,' she says.

'But the Castle's the best place we ever lived in,' I say. Even though it's a lie. Gran's was better.

She's staring at me but I don't think she's really seeing me. It's like she's looking through me. The same as the people on the streets. Like I'm invisible. But it's different. Cos they see nothing when they're looking through me. Right now, though, Ma's seeing something. I can tell.

67

I remember that look. I've seen it before.

It's the same look I saw on Gran's face when Ma was dragging me away from her house. Like she'd been walking all day and had just realized she'd taken a wrong turn and was back where she started.

Ma walks away and plonks herself down on the couch.

I don't know what to say so I just say, 'Ma,' which doesn't help, cos she looks up like she's waiting for me to say something to make her feel better and I just stand there.

She shoves her thumbs into her eyes. 'This is all wrong. All wrong. Got to move on.' She's not talking to me, though. She's talking to herself.

I'm so dumb. It's been one year and eight months since we found this place. One year and eight months since they almost got me. And not once has Ma got stressed out. Not once has she got drunk. Or worse.

'Don't be stressed, Ma, it's okay,' I say, and I go over and sit down beside her. I rest my head on her shoulder. 'The Castle's deadly, Ma. It's huge. It's ours. And it has a moat.' I point to the canal. 'No one can get in.'

'Or out,' she says. She puts her arm around me.

"Zactly. You promised you'd find me a castle and I promised I'd never leave.' I nod. Cos it was a deal.

After ages has passed, Ma takes her arm away. I want to ask her what that look meant. But I can't. Cos she won't know what I'm talking about and I don't know how to explain. The words would come out all wrong and it'd probably stress her out more. So I stay quiet.

68

I want to see her eyes so I lean forwards. But when I do, I nearly gasp.

They're as deep as the canal.

'Ma?'

Ma stands up. She bites her nails. 'I'm going out.'

'No, Ma!' I say. I don't want her going out there with her eyes like that. Cos I know what that means.

She gives me a watery smile. 'Relax, I'll be back, I promise,' she says. Then her smile melts away. 'Stay here, yeah? Don't go out.'

I nod.

Then Ma empties half of the begging cup into her hand and turns and walks into the kitchen.

A SICK MOON

They were real loud, the men that turned up on the beach that night. Shouting and laughing. There were five of them. Maybe six. They were carrying plastic bags and they sat down on the sand and started drinking from cans. Ma didn't know them cos she didn't say hi or anything.

'Ma, I'm hungry,' I said, cos I didn't want to be there any more, listening to those men. It was getting dark anyway so we walked back up to the tent and grabbed our plastic bottles for getting water. We carried them to the tap in the shipyard behind the harbour wall to fill them. I brought the small one back and Ma took the big one. The small one was for drinking and the big one was for washing.

We ate some bread and those blocks of cheese where you tear off the wax coat and inside they look like little wheels. Then I brushed my teeth and got into my pyjamas. I was real tired then, so we climbed into the tent and I pulled the sleeping bag around me, and I didn't ask Ma when we were going back to Gran's. Instead I asked her to tell me a story about a castle.

Ma made sure my sleeping bag was zipped up tight and then she said, 'There once was a princess who lived in a castle. 'Cept she didn't know she was a princess.'

'Why not?'

'Cos no one had ever told her.' She paused for dramatic effect. Then she said, 'The princess didn't know that she lived in a castle neither.'

'How could she not know?'

'Cos it was old and run-down and she'd never lived anywhere else. How could she know it was a castle and not just an ordinary house if she had never seen or been anywhere else?'

'Why didn't her friends tell her?'

'She didn't have any friends. Just a harp that sang when the princess played it.'

'Oh,' I said. I wanted to ask why the princess had never been anywhere else but my head was starting to get all droopy.

'There was an old forest around the castle. And the trees had scars where branches used to grow. And in the scars were eyes.' She made another pause for dramatic effect.

'If the princess went for a walk, the eyes of the trees would follow her . . .'

I thought that was cool. It was real creepy. But I don't know what happened to the princess cos while she was wandering through the forest I fell asleep. And I never found out what the Moral was cos when I woke up, there were voices outside the tent. I could hear Ma too. But now she sounded like she was playing that game where you chew a biscuit and then try to talk without spraying crumbs everywhere. And I knew that meant she was drunk.

Ma must've invited the men on the beach up to our tent. I couldn't believe it. How could she? It was our dune. There weren't supposed to be other people in it.

They had lit a fire. I could see their shadows on the side of the tent. Then I felt the twang of someone tripping over the rope of the tent. Something came crashing into the side of it. It was squashing me. The whole tent was bending. I squeezed out from under it and unzipped the door.

That's when I saw him.

A huge man. He'd fallen into the side of the tent. Everyone was breaking their hearts laughing. One guy tried to help him get up, but the huge man fell back down again. He dragged the other guy with him till they were both lying on the side of the tent. I heard the snap of the centre pole breaking.

Then he stood up. The sound of his laugh mixed with the spitting of the fire.

I jumped back.

He had three eyebrows cos one was cut in half by a scar. He was tall. Square shoulders, so big they almost touched his ears. His hair was as red as the fire's flames and his skin as white as the foam on the waves. He was an evil red devil monkey.

And Ma was laughing along with him. They all were.

He was massive compared to the others. They just looked like hungry chickens, all stooped over and cackling, with their eyes darting all over the place.

My eyes started stinging. I turned cos I didn't want them to see me crying. I ran away and I was halfway to the harbour wall when Ma caught me.

'Here, stop – what are you doing?' she said, and she grabbed a handful of my pyjamas.

'What are *you* doing, Ma?' I said and I wiped my eyes so she wouldn't see me crying cos I knew she'd tell me I was being silly.

'Nothing, just having a laugh with a few mates.'

She tried to take my arm but I pulled away. 'They're not your mates, Ma.'

'They are now,' she said, real happy with herself. 'Ah, come on, don't be silly.'

'I don't want to be here any more, Ma.' And I didn't. Cos Ma and her new mates had ruined it. 'I want to be in Gran's house.'

'Ah, love, they're only having a few cans. It's Saturday night.'

But I didn't see what Saturday had to do with it. 'I don't want to be here any more.'

'What are you talking about? You love the beach. And we had a laugh today, didn't we?'

I didn't answer her.

'Look, I'm sorry about the tent. I'll get us a new one tomorrow – a bigger one.'

I didn't care about the tent. I didn't want a bigger one.

'Come on, you can't stay out here. It's late. Just go back to sleep and we'll fix the tent in the morning, okay?'

'Can we go back to Gran's tomorrow?' I asked.

But then Ma's voice went all hard, the way it goes when she's had enough. 'Look, don't start stressing me out, okay? I've enough going on. I just needed to relax, all right?' I didn't answer cos it didn't make sense. She'd spent the whole day relaxing on the beach. 'I'll get them to move so you can sleep, okay?' She meant Monkey Man and the chickens. 'They're leaving soon anyway. Now come on, stop whinging, all right?'

Ma grabbed my hand and I tried to pull away but Ma's real strong. She dragged me back to the tent, even though I kept saying I didn't want to go. When we got there, Monkey Man was standing over it and he'd tied something to the top.

'Just like new!' he said, and he smiled. But it wasn't a nice smile.

'See?' Ma said. 'All fixed! Now, lads, do yis mind if we move away from the tent so madam here can get some sleep?'

They all started standing up and saying, 'Not a bother,' and they went off down the beach. Ma looked at me real proud, like she'd just made everything all better, but then she left too. I didn't know what she meant by 'madam' but she said it in the same voice she used to tell me I was being silly. It made me want to shout at her. But I didn't say anything, cos there was no point. There never was when Ma had been drinking.

I just crawled back into the tent where the poles were

broken and the side was all floppy. I lay there for ages trying to sleep. But I couldn't cos every time I heard the wind moving through the grass, I thought it was Monkey Man crawling around outside, glowing like a sick moon.

I couldn't believe Ma would bring them to our dune. I was so angry that it stung my fingers and toes. I hated her and her stupid laugh and her stupid drinking.

I still wished that she was there with me, though.

But even when it started getting light, I could hear her laughing from the beach.

SARDINES AND CAKE

I'm sitting in the backyard with two slices of birthday cake in my hand. Ma's gone out. Into the streets. With eyes as deep as the canal.

She says she'll be back. She promised. And Ma always comes back. But I still feel like a bag of spiders is crawling around inside me.

I take the blanket that's drying off the line and fold it nice. I put a clothes peg on it and the slices of cake and I pick up the bar of soap that Ma was using. It's already dry on the top so I put it on the blanket with the dry part facing down and I go inside.

I sneak up beneath the window in the basement that looks into the space where Caretaker lives. I climb up onto the windowsill and peek over the boards.

Below me is Caretaker and his trolley and his books and his blankets. I can't see him. All I can see is a massive heap of blankets against the wall. But the shape of the heap tells me he's in there. On my left, behind his head, there's a wall, and it's real important cos when there's a storm, the canal sometimes floods, and the wall stops the water coming in and drowning Caretaker.

Caretaker likes lots of blankets cos he doesn't like being wet. Even on a windy day, when the rain is slanty and comes in off the street, he stays dry. Cos even if the top few blankets get wet, it'd be impossible for the water to get through every single blanket.

'Whoooooo . . .' I say through the gap in the window and I make my voice all breezy so that I sound like a ghost. 'I am the ghost of the mill. I bring you soap.' I drop the bar of soap onto the outside window ledge and then whip my head back in and crouch beneath the boards.

After a while I lift myself up high enough to see. The soap is still there.

'Whoooooo . . .' I say. 'You must waaaaaash.'

I duck down again and wait. But when I get up, the bar is still there. So this time I drop the slice of chocolate cake on the windowsill beside the bar of soap and I hide and wait a while and when I finally take a peek, the soap is still there but the cake is gone and there are crumbs all over the blankets.

I climb through the gap in the window and I take the blanket and the peg and the other slice of cake with me. I jump down and sit close to Caretaker, but not too close, and I pinch the peg on my nose and I say in my normal voice, 'I brought you a blanket.' Except that it's not my normal voice, it sounds all funny cos of the peg. 'Ma *washed* it,' I say, and I say 'washed' slowly so he might get the point.

A hand appears from the blankets. The fingernails are almost as long as Ma's but they're all black with dirt. The hand pushes back the blankets and now I can see a bird's nest. But I know it's not, it just looks like the swallows' nest that's above the window on the sixth floor. It's really Caretaker's beard. He throws back a few more blankets and sits up.

Caretaker is wearing sunglasses with one lens, and he squints at me with his free eye. He's only wearing one hat today. It's brown and has a wide rim, like a jungle explorer's hat. I wonder if it belonged to the same explorer who owned my new binoculars.

He takes the blanket I brought like it's a handful of eggs and strokes the material and says, 'Not a thing wrong with that. Not a thing.' He puts it on top of a stack of blankets that's so high it wobbles and nearly tips over.

'I think Ma got it from a Do-gooder the other day,' I say. 'Or maybe from the skip.'

Feet pass by on the street above us. Caretaker's books are all lined up on the pavement. People can buy books from him or swap their own with one of Caretaker's for a few coins.

'It's my birthday,' I say, to point out the fact that it's him that should be bringing *me* presents, and not the other way round.

'Is it now?' he says.

'Ma got me a present.'

He lifts an eyebrow and I hold up the binoculars, which are hanging around my neck.

He nods. 'Good present. Practical.'

'I agree,' I say, though I don't actually know what 'practical' means. Maybe it means you need to practise to be able to use it properly. Like a basketball.

A woman stops on the pavement and bends over and looks at the books.

'When's your birthday?' I ask.

'I dunno,' he says.

'What do you mean, you don't know?' I ask. 'Everyone knows their own birthday, don't they?'

'I forgot mine,' he says.

The woman on the street chooses a book, drops a coin into his cup, and moves on. Caretaker cranes his head up. I think he's trying to see which book she took. 'Business is booming,' he says, like it's a bad thing. 'They only choose the rubbish, mind. *Ulysses* has been there for years.' Then he leans back and pulls a blanket around him. He must be roasting under there.

He takes out a tin of sardines and pulls it open.

'How could you forget your own birthday?' I ask.

He scrunches up his nose like he can smell himself. 'Cos it's not important,' he says, and he shoves some fish in his mouth and oil drips off his fingers onto the blankets.

'Yes, it is!'

'Why?' he asks with his mouth full.

'Cos . . . !'

I don't know what else to say. It's not something I ever thought needed explaining before. 'It's yours and no one else's!' I say in the end.

Caretaker just shakes his head and swallows. 'That doesn't matter,' he says. He wipes his lips with his sleeve and I stay quiet, cos Caretaker is weird and I don't know how to explain to him that it *does* matter.

Then he says, 'When's your death day?'

And that doesn't make any sense. 'How can I know that?' I ask and he shrugs.

Then he looks straight at me with his one eye. 'But seems like a more important question, don't you think? Birthday, bleugh!' He flicks his greasy fingers at me. 'But today and your death day and the time in between. Now –' And he points a dirty finger at me – 'that's worth thinking about.'

He stares at me for ages, as if he wants me to agree. Sometimes I wonder if he's away with the fairies.

He wipes his fingers on the blankets and reaches up and grabs a book and opens it. I look at my slice of cake but I don't want it. I hand it to him and he takes it without looking at me and shoves it in his mouth. Sardines and cake. Gross.

The peg hurts my nose and I take it off. But then the smell hits me. It's like the juice in the bottom of the bin when you take out a full bag and you realize that the bag has ripped and the bottom of the bin is full of liquid that's leaked out.

'Phew, you really smell!' I say.

Caretaker ignores me.

'Why don't you wash?' I ask.

'Don't like getting wet,' he says.

'But you smell like a bin,' I say.

He looks down at himself and sniffs the air a few times. 'I can't smell anything,' he says.

'But *I* can!'

He lowers the book and looks at me. 'Well,' he says, 'that would seem to me to be distinctly your problem.' And then he lifts the book again.

I'm about to say something about it being the world's problem at this stage, but I stop. Instead I say, 'Caretaker? You believe in ghosts?'

He looks at me and his face is flat. He says, 'You believe in memories?'

'Yeah,' I say, 'of course. But that's not the same thing.'

'Isn't it?'

'No,' I say, and I'm pretty sure I'm right so I go on. 'It's not the same. I'm talking about *actual* ghosts.'

'Ghosts can't exist without people. Without people and their pasts and their memories.'

But he's just waffling now so I try to make my face go like Ma's egg-sucking face to show him that I'm not impressed.

Caretaker sighs, like he's tired of having to talk to idiots, and he says, 'Seems there's more ghosts than people in this city.'

I think that means he does believe in ghosts. 'Are they good or bad?'

'Are *people* good or bad?' he asks.

I shrug. 'Both.'

"Zactly,' he says, and he starts reading again.

I'm playing with the peg and one side of it pops out of the metal spring. 'I think the mill is haunted by a ghost that drags its mangled body around,' I say. I'm trying to stretch the metal bits apart so I can slide the plastic arm of the peg back in. But it breaks and the metal spring flies away onto Caretaker's blanket.

He's staring at me with the weirdest look on his face.

'What?' I say. I think I just scared him. 'I don't mean it! I haven't seen it. Anyway, Ma says I'm just making it up and she's right, I probably am. She says I've got an overactive imagination.'

He keeps looking at me.

'Don't be scared, Caretaker,' I say.

'No. I'm not scared,' he says.

That's when I realize. His weird look. It's not cos he's scared.

He's sad.

His eye has gone all big and deep. Like Ma's.

'Sorry,' I say but that doesn't help.

I still want to know if he knows anything about the coins, though, so I ask, 'Have you ever seen anything weird going on here? Not ghosts but just, I dunno, weird stuff?'

He's not saying anything. His mouth is hanging open. He stays quiet for real long. I stand up but he doesn't notice.

'Caretaker?'

He says nothing.

Great. I've made Caretaker sad. And I've stressed out Ma.

I think of her sitting on the couch looking like she'd been punched. And then I think of her lying in a doorway somewhere with dead eyes, and then I don't want to think about it any more.

I want her to come home. I'm going to the roof to look for her.

STANDING GUARD

I'm passing the second floor, the one with the dead machines. There's a noise. A scuffling sound. My eyes dart over the room. I see something. Beside one of the machines. On the floor. It's white and grey. It's moving.

I step forwards into the room. There's another shuffling sound. I stop. It's quiet. I take another step.

Something comes flying out at me, like the witch coming flying round the altar! I scream. It's coming for my face!

Then it drops down. And shivers. And settles its feathers. It's just a pigeon.

'You'd swear it was the first time I've seen a bleeding pigeon,' I say.

It flies again and then lands fatly on a fallen machine. It looks at me with its dumb eyes.

'What?' I say, but it just sits there and coos.

Pigeons are real stupid. Seagulls are smarter. They know

how to grab a piece of bread straight out of your hand and fly away before you can chuck a stone at them. But pigeons sit around asking to be kicked. I seen the boys in the wetsuits do it.

I walk up to the pigeon and he's still cooing away, so I shoo him with my hand and he flies over to the empty window, the one that fell in during the storm last year. I get real close and start flapping my arms like mad and he still doesn't move, so I run straight at him and finally he cops on and flies out.

'Stupid pigeon.'

Maybe Ma was right. Maybe the sound was just a pigeon.

There are two girls walking over the bridge. They're around my age. They're in school uniforms with white shirts and grey skirts. Why do school uniforms always look so boring? Why can't the skirts be pink or have stripes or dots or something?

Both of the girls have real long hair, like Rapunzel, and it looks like they've got ribbons in their plaits. One has a pink ribbon and one has a blue ribbon. The plaits hang almost all the way down to their waists.

The girls are walking towards a group of boys in wetsuits that are standing by the railing of the bridge. They must know them, cos one of the boys is shouting at them and the girls have stopped talking to each other and are looking at the boys. The boy who was shouting comes close. He's real tall. He grabs the one with the pink plait and shoves her towards the railing and she's screaming, I can hear her from here. I think he's trying to throw her into the water.

The other girl is shouting at the boys but they're all just laughing and Pink Plait is halfway over the railing now and she's hitting the tall boy's head, but I don't think he cares cos he's laughing like mad.

But now Blue Plait is holding something over the railings. I think it's a bag. Maybe it belongs to the tall boy, cos he's stopped laughing and he's staring at Blue Plait and she's staring back at him and shaking the bag over the water. After a minute he lets go of Pink Plait and she goes running back to her friend.

Now the girls are walking together straight through the group of boys. The boys are pretending to grab the girls, but Blue Plait is still holding the bag over the water so the boys don't actually try to throw the girls into the canal again – they're just messing. When they get past the boys, Blue Plait throws the bag back and then grabs the other girl's hand and they run away.

But when they get to the other side of the bridge, they stop and they turn and they both give the finger to the group of boys, and now it's the girls who are laughing and I laugh too.

I look down at my hair. It's loose and messy. I can't remember the last time I brushed it. I never plait it. And I don't have any ribbons.

Ma still isn't home.

I see Red Coat. With the binoculars, I can see her face

much better. She's real nice-looking. I nearly missed her cos she's on her own. He's not with her. She's one of loads of people moving over the bridge. I follow her till I can't see her any more. Then I keep on looking, till all the people are gone and the streets are quiet.

Ma still isn't home.

On the canal there are lots of boats and people live on them. I think it'd be cool to live on a boat cos you've got water all around you, like a castle with a moat. The boats even have planks of wood that you have to walk over to get on and off, and they're like drawbridges cos you can lift them up and float away and no one can get onto your boat. So you'd be safe.

There's one boat that's green with a red line painted around it. I can see through the windows with the binoculars. There's a woman. She's almost naked except she's got trousers on and she's holding a baby to her chest. I think she's trying to feed it but the baby's going mental crying. Its face is all red and scrunched up. I bet it's roaring so loud that people walking along the bank can hear it.

Actually I think the woman is crying too. She keeps trying to feed the baby but it's kicking its legs and shaking its head so I don't think it's hungry. Maybe it's angry cos its ma's tears are dripping on its head.

Some swans float past the boat. There's a ma and dad swan, and three babies. There used to be five. But the seagulls swooped down and grabbed the other two when they were still real small. I seen them do it. The three babies that are left are bigger now, though, even bigger than the seagulls. So I don't think the seagulls could take them.

It must be real hard for the ma and dad to watch their babies being taken and not be able to do anything to stop it. They must hate seagulls.

I point the binoculars above the boat, real high, right to the top of an apartment building, and I can see a woman and a man through a window that takes up the whole wall.

They're in the kitchen, at least I think it's the kitchen cos there are pots and pans hanging from a silver bar on the wall, but there's no bucket for washing. They do have a tap, though. It's inside, not outside on the wall.

The kitchen's all white and gleaming and looks real nice. But she doesn't look nice, she looks mean. She's pretty – even prettier than Ma – and her clothes look dead posh, like it's the first time they've ever been worn. But she's real skinny. If I had money, there's no way I'd be that skinny. I'd eat curry chips and a battered sausage for lunch and dinner every day.

Her face is as red as the baby on the boat. She looks like she's shouting at the man. He's standing on the other side of this table that's real high, and the chairs around it are real high too, and I think it's made of white stone, though I don't know if stone can be white.

He has one hand on his hip and he's stabbing the air with the other hand. And now she picks up a funny-shaped glass and throws it right at a clock and it smashes and red wine spreads down the wall like blood and he's marching away out the front door and I imagine I can hear the door slam.

The skinny woman storms out of the room and into another. There's a kid in there. She's real young, around four or something. Her room is white. The wardrobe and the rugs and the bed are all pure white. But the kid's got a red crayon and she's drawing right in the middle of a big white wall. I don't know what she's drawing. Maybe it's a bear or something. It's not very good. But I agree with the kid, it's better than white. I don't think the ma agrees, though, cos she's shouting and the kid drops the crayon and shoves its hand in its mouth. The ma grabs the crayon off the ground and throws it back into a box. Then she takes a remote off a white table and she clicks on this huge TV and picks up the kid and drops her down in front of it. She's still shouting at her when she marches back out of the room.

I follow her through the sitting room into the kitchen. She gets to this tall silver bin and dumps the box of crayons inside.

These binoculars are great.

I lower them and it takes me a second to recognize Ma. She's coming over the bridge. I try to look at her face but she keeps bumping around. So instead I run over the roof and down the ladder and across the sky-bridge and through the mill. I hear her knock just as I get to the basement.

I unlock the door. 'Hey Ma,' I say.

She's been leaning on the door and stumbles as I open it. She laughs. 'Heya, love,' she says, and bends down and kisses me. And that's when it hits me. Her sour breath.

The bag of spiders in my stomach explodes. They crawl

out, hundreds of them, and they swarm through my veins and up my neck and into my brain.

'Ma?' I step back.

She's still bending over me, wobbling. 'You didn't go out, did ye?'

I shake my head.

'And I came back, didn't I?' she says. 'Just like I said I would.' She stands up straight. 'I'll never leave you. Never, never, never,' she says. But she's not looking at me. She's looking into the shadows.

'Ma?'

I can't believe she's drunk. She promised.

'I promised,' she says like she can hear me thinking. But then she says, 'Promised I'd come back.'

She pushes past me and I watch her go into the kitchen.

I thought Ma had changed. I thought she was better.

A FREE RIDE

The morning after Monkey Man broke our tent, the Authorities arrived. Back then I didn't know about them. I knew about cops and stuff, I just didn't know I was supposed to be scared of them.

At first, when I heard them outside the tent, I thought they were the men from the night before.

'Hello? Anyone in there?'

I gave Ma a dig but she just groaned. Then the zip on the tent started opening so I kicked Ma. She said, 'What?' like she was real annoyed with me for waking her up.

But the Authorities had heard too and they said, 'Come on out here.'

Ma woke up properly then. She sat up and yelled, 'Hold on a sec!' Then she gave me her egg-sucking face and said, 'It's the coppers. Not a word out of you.'

She threw off her sleeping bag and crawled over to the zip and stuck her head out. 'Morning,' she said.

I could see two sets of legs outside. Both wearing navy trousers. One was crouching down and he was wearing a neon yellow jacket. He used a stick or something to hold back the zipper so he could see past Ma. He saw me, and he nodded and then he stood up.

Ma crawled out and she stood up too.

'Bit of a party here last night?' one of the coppers asked.

'Was there?' Ma said. 'Oh yeah, think there were some lads messing around here last night. They're gone now, though.'

'Is that right?' one of the coppers said. 'Living here, are you?'

I saw Ma move from one leg to the other. 'Ah no. Just camped here last night,' which was a lie. We'd been there for weeks.

No one said anything for a while. I heard Ma sniffing and one of the policemen walking around, kicking cans. Finally the one beside Ma said, 'How long have you been living here?'

'We're not living here. Just the one night, that's all.' Ma sniffed again and shoved her hands in her pockets. 'Went for a swim and camped last night. She's mad for the camping, so she is, and the weather was good so we stayed. Bit of an adventure, ye know?'

'Right,' he said but you could tell he didn't believe her. 'So where *are* you living, if it's not here?' I heard the other one kick a can again. And that's when Ma gave them Gran's address.

'Is that right?' he said. 'Sure I'll give you a lift back there, then.'

'Ah, no need. We'll walk,' Ma said. 'It's a nice morning. Might take a swim first.'

The coppers were quiet for a while. I heard them shuffle around. Ma walked away from the tent too and they talked, but I couldn't hear what they were saying.

Then she was back and one of the coppers said, 'Right. Well, I don't want to see you back here tonight, all right?'

'Yeah, 'course,' Ma said.

When they were gone, Ma stuck her head back inside and said, 'Time to go.'

We packed up her rucksack but we left the empty cans and water bottles and broken tent where they were and started walking back to the road.

I kept asking Ma if we really were going back to Gran's. She wouldn't answer. But then we got on a bus that crossed the whole city. I didn't know where we were going. But I knew it was nowhere near Gran's.

So I stopped asking.

PART

TWO

THE DIRTY SPY

It's been over three weeks since Ma started drinking again. We are running out of gas and it's real expensive. But she's spent everything. Right now I'm making tea with whatever is left in the gas bottle and trying not to bang the pots too much.

'Jaysus, me head,' Ma says and she pushes an ashtray that's full of cigarette butts over to the other side of the table. She sits down and shoves her face into her hands.

I wait till the pot is spluttering, then I turn off the heat and put in three teabags and cover it with a lid that's much too big. I put it on the table.

Ma only drinks tea that's real black. She says it should be so strong that a spoon could stand up straight in it. But I tried that before and it doesn't work. Even with a whole box of teabags in the pot. And then Ma went mad at me for wasting perfectly good tea.

I pick up a long red piece of material. I tore it off one of my old T-shirts. Ma went mad at me for wrecking a perfectly good T-shirt too, but it was dead old anyway. I wrap it around my head and tie it at the back, but I leave one part real long. Then I split my hair into three parts and plait the red material into my hair. The bottom of the plait doesn't reach my waist like the schoolgirls' hair did. I wouldn't make a very good Rapunzel. But it goes halfway down my back, which is pretty good.

I look at Ma but she's still got her head down. I don't think the tea is black enough for her yet. There are empty cans of beer all over the kitchen. She must have been up all night.

I go around picking the cans up and putting them in a plastic bag. I see the begging cup that's sitting in the corner on the ground and I look into it. It's empty and I'm worried. I haven't been able to get my hands on any coins for the last few weeks cos Ma keeps spending everything. Yesterday was the first time I managed to nick some without Ma noticing.

'We need gas, Ma,' I say.

She doesn't answer.

'And batteries for the torches and the lights.'

Still nothing.

'Ma,' I say.

'I know, I heard ye.'

I open the door and chuck the bag of cans outside and close it quickly again cos it's freezing out there, even though it's only the end of October. I sit down at the table with Ma and pour the tea and add the last of the milk. I haven't had hot food in ages but I don't say it to Ma cos that'll just give her an excuse to go out again, and she'll forget to get me food anyway and she'll spend the money on drink. I don't need a battered sausage and chips that much.

'I finished all those sums,' I tell her.

She lifts her head and opens her eyes a tiny bit and from the way she's squinting, you'd swear there were a hundred trucks blaring their horns in our kitchen. She lifts her cup but spills a bit cos her hands are shaking. She takes a sip. 'Jaysus,' she says. Then she says, 'What?'

'Maths,' I say. 'You left me homework yesterday.'

Actually it wasn't yesterday, it was two days ago. She was drinking all day yesterday so I had to teach myself and I never choose maths if I don't have to. Instead I chose art.

I'm drawing on the walls of the basement. The whole room. Pictures of trees with eyes that follow you, and mountains and a drawbridge and a moat. Everything you'd see out of the windows of a castle. I don't have any colours, but I've loads and loads of black paint and old brushes that we found in the skip.

'Will you go through them?' I ask. She squints at me. She's already forgotten what we're talking about. 'My homework, the sums – will you correct them today?'

Maybe she won't drink today. Maybe she'll come to the classroom and teach me.

'Yeah,' she says. 'In a bit.' She takes another sip of tea. Then she puts her head in her hands and groans again.

'Hungover?' I ask, real sarcastic.

'A little. But it was only cans,' she says, and what she means is that drinking cans is hardly drinking at all so I should stop nagging her. In a way, I know she's right. I shouldn't stress her out cos it could be worse. A lot worse.

But it could be better too.

There's steam coming off my tea. I lift the cup to my mouth and I make a hole with my lips that's the size of a pea and I suck tea in through it and it makes a slurping sound.

'Don't,' Ma says.

I spit the tea back into the cup. I lick my teeth and remember that I forgot to brush them cos they feel all furry. Ma looks up at me like she's surprised I'm still here. 'Go on upstairs and read your history book,' she says. 'I'll be up in a minute.' She drops her head again.

I take another mouthful of tea and swirl it around. I look at the top of Ma's head. Her hair's greasy and her parting's all wobbly. She needs a wash.

I spit the tea out again but Ma doesn't say anything. 'Coming up?' I ask.

'Yeah.'

'Promise?'

She looks at me. 'I said *yeah*. Now go on, move it!'

I leave my tea. I don't want it anyway. I head upstairs. But even before I've gotten to the classroom, before I've even reached the first floor, I hear the *k-tiss* of a can being opened and I know Ma's drinking again.

*

Ma comes into the classroom a while later. She stinks of beer and cigarettes. But when I turn to look at her, her eyes seem clear enough. For now.

'What's that?' she asks, and nods her head at my copybook.

'It's a drawing of a praying mantis.' I point at the picture of the insect in the book.

'A what?'

'A praying mantis. It's an insect found in warm countries. He gets his name cos he has real long legs that he holds out in front of him and it looks like he's praying, and he's a carnivore, which means he eats other insects.' I say all that without even looking at the book cos I just remember it all. Then I point to the pictures on the wall. There are loads of praying mantises stuck up there now. The holes in the plaster on the walls don't look like chickenpox any more cos instead it looks like the praying mantises have been eating it.

Ma lifts the book and turns it so she can see the cover and then she says, 'What else have you learned?'

I tell her that pandas mostly eat leaves, and that camels have long eyelashes cos of the sandstorms, and that there are no penguins in the North Pole, only the South Pole. When I'm finished, Ma's rubbing her forehead between her finger and thumb but she's smiling a little bit too.

'You're some woman for one woman, missus,' she says, and she puts her hand on the back of my neck and it's freezing but I don't flinch or pull away. She rests her chin on my head and says nothing for a while. I tilt my head back and she leans forwards till our foreheads are touching, upside down. Then she stands straight and she claps her hands together and says, 'Right, show us them sums.'

I lift up my book and bury my face in it, cos I don't want her to see that I'm smiling.

Ma sits with me for three full hours before she goes out, and I make her promise she'll be home early and that she'll bring me a bag of chips and a battered sausage, and she says she will, that she's only going out begging for money for gas.

The mill's real quiet now. I stand up and leave my books on the table and go downstairs to the basement. In the corner beneath the stairs is a loose stone. I jerk it from side to side till it comes out and behind it is a cardboard coffee cup that's torn around the edges. I put it in here yesterday when I finally managed to nick some coins from Ma. I slide it out and look inside. A few euro coins and some coppers. I leave the euros behind and just take the coppers, cos we need the money and if there is a ghost, I don't think it cares what coins I use.

I put down coins on the first three floors, just like I did the other time. But I don't go up to the periscope on the fourth floor to listen. This time I take a few deep breaths and I force myself to go back onto the second floor and I crouch behind the first of the dead machines, the one closest to the door.

I wait for ages and ages but nothing happens, I'm just getting cold. I stay where I am for ages more. Nothing moves. I don't see anything and I don't hear anything. All the coins are where I left them. All five of them. Maybe it only works when I'm not here. Or maybe it doesn't work any more.

I can hear a crane clattering outside but nothing else. No ghost shuffling around or anything. 'Of course there's no bleeding ghost shuffling around,' I say. 'Cos there's no bleeding ghost.'

I don't know how I feel. I think I'm relieved. I need to pee but I don't want to go downstairs. I stand up and look around. The dust moves a little in the breeze that's coming in through the gaps but that's all. I'm bored and stiff.

I go to the end of the room where there are plastic bowling pins all over the place. Ma got them from a charity shop too. I collect them up and stand them in a triangle and then I look for the foam ball, which I can't find at first but eventually see all the way back by the door.

The trick is to roll the ball to the right a bit, cos there's a slant in the floor, but I roll it too far to the right and I completely miss the pins. The next time is better – I hit three. But it's not very good. One time I got five strikes in a row. Ma's only ever gotten one.

I fix the three pins and turn to walk back.

Shuffle, shuffle, shuffle, stop.

It can't be.

Shuffle, shuffle, shuffle, stop.

It's here. It's back again.

Shuffle, shuffle, shuffle, stop.

I don't believe it. This can't be happening.

Shuffle, shuffle, shuffle, stop.

Thump, thump, thump.

It's climbing the stairs. It's real.

Thump, thump, thump.

I should run. It's going to grab me and kill me and there's no one here to help. What am I doing in here?

Thump, thump, thump.

There's nowhere to go. I'm trapped.

It's finished climbing. It's outside the bedroom. I see a shoe!

I turn. Sprint across the room. But there's no time. I reach the fourth pillar, run behind it and dive to the ground. My face is in the dirt. I'm breathing it in. I'm going to cough. I put my hand over my mouth.

Shuffle, shuffle, shuffle, stop.

It's coming for me! I can't look.

There's a tinkling sound and a jingling sound and then . . .

Shuffle, shuffle, shuffle.

There's a bang from the building site outside. Life's still going on like normal out there, like there isn't a ghost dragging its mangled body through the room.

I let out a tiny sound. It's heard me now.

Shuffle, shuffle, shuffle, stop.

It's in front of me. It's at the machine, I know it is. I lift my arm a tiny bit. I open one eye. Through the dust I can see the machine. There's something moving out from behind it. Moving towards me. It has massive black feet and feathers dragging off the ground and hair all over and it's groaning a little and it's going to grab me and eat me and—

'Caretaker!' I yell.

I can't believe it! It's Caretaker! Of course it is, he reeks – I can smell bin juice from here! I'm up on my feet and I try to run out from behind the pillar but my legs are too wobbly. I hug it instead.

Caretaker lifts the coin off the machine, holds it up to the light and turns it over a few times. Then he drops it in his pocket where it jingles. Finally he looks at me. It's like this is the first time he's noticed me. And he doesn't care that I'm standing right here watching him nick my coins. He looks at me and then turns and he starts shuffling again!

I watch him move. His long coat is torn at the bottom and it's dragging off the ground. It does look like feathers. It really does.

He gets to the last machine and he does the same thing. He picks up the coin and he looks at it and he puts it in his pocket.

Caretaker is the ghost and he's nicking my coins! I burst out laughing. It explodes through the room. It bounces off the walls and soaks into the floors.

He turns round and shuffles towards me, then past me and right out of the room. I hear the *thump, thump, thump* as he climbs up to the next floor.

I wish Ma was here now so I could tell her that everything's all right. There *is* no ghost. The Castle is safe!

Caretaker is shuffling through the room above me, I can hear him. I take a load of deep breaths and try to stop laughing. I walk out towards the stairs. Above me, Caretaker is doing the same – he's walking towards the stairs. When I get to the hall and look up, though, I hear the *thump, thump, thump* of Caretaker climbing up, not down. The smell of him is still in the stairway.

What is he doing? He never comes in here, inside the mill! How did he even get in here? The door downstairs is locked, it's always locked. And how did he know I'd put out the coins?

I wait and listen. I can't believe Caretaker has been stealing my coins. Why didn't he just ask me? I'd give him some. They're only coppers anyway.

I hear him come back downstairs and I stand there as he passes me. He hardly even looks at me. He goes on down the stairs and I hear my coins jingling in his pockets, but then I see something else too. There's a chain at his hip holding lots of keys. I run down the stairs behind him.

'Caretaker!'

He doesn't stop and he doesn't turn round, he just keeps walking through the basement.

'Caretaker!' I yell again, and then I run in front of him and I turn round and walk backwards so I'm facing him. 'What are you doing?'

'Leaving,' he says.

'I know that. But, well, you took my coins!'

He nods and says, 'Left them out for me.'

I'm about to say that I didn't but then I stop. Does he really think I was leaving them out for him? 'But how did you know? That they were there?'

'Can see them,' he says, and he nods towards the basement window.

I look at the window and picture Caretaker on his tippy-toes looking through the gap over the boards. The old spy! 'But why didn't you just ask me for them?'

But then he gives me this strange look. 'She leaves them out for me.'

I feel a tingle run up my spine and I think of Ma saying, 'Someone just walked over me grave', and I think I know what she means. She means something weird is going on. 'Who?'

Caretaker keeps walking towards me. '*She* does,' he says, and he's not talking about me.

Now I want to laugh again. I think he's messing with me, cos he knew I thought there was a ghost. But I don't laugh. Cos he's serious. 'Caretaker, there is no ghost. Why do you think there's a ghost?'

But then I remember that I told him that the mill was haunted. 'Oh no, Caretaker. There is no ghost. It was me. I left out the coins.' I feel a bit bad cos it's like I've tricked him. 'I'm sorry, Caretaker.'

Caretaker smiles at me. He's real close now so I stand to one side cos I'm not brave enough to stand in Caretaker's way. When he gets to the door, he doesn't look at me. He just says, 'Long before your time, kiddo,' and he chooses a key from the bunch at his hip and opens the door. The light blinds me. Caretaker shuffles down the steps and starts walking along the street.

'Caretaker!' I call, and I take a few steps but then the sunlight hits me. It's so loud out here. There are people walking and cranes banging. The traffic is stuck cos of the lights at the end of the street. There's a woman driving a car with a tiny kid in a chair in the back, and he looks at me.

I'm outside. People could see me.

I jump back real quick but the lights have changed. The kid's head turns towards me as the car starts to move. But that's okay, he's too young to matter and I don't think anyone else noticed me.

CONCRETE CITY

The next place we stayed after the beach was in this flat on the third floor of a big building. The building was the same dull colour as the concrete yard outside, where all the kids played. In the middle of the yard was a yellow slide and a yellow climbing frame. When you looked out the window of the flat, you could see another building that was the exact same, with grey washing hanging on every balcony. And off to one side, in the space between the next block of flats, was a huge electricity pylon.

We were staying with a mate of Ma's. She had two kids. One was a boy called Mark. He was my age but he was really weird. He kept shoving everything he found on the ground into his mouth. But he was nice. He let me share his half-chewed crayons and when we ran out of paper, we drew on the walls of his bedroom. His ma didn't care.

The other kid was a baby and she was real annoying cos she never stopped crying and she was always covered in snot and her nappy was always stinking. I remember one day Mark's ma wheeled the baby into his room in this buggy that only had three good wheels and one that wobbled like mad when you tried to push it.

'Here, Mark, go out and play. And take your sister with ye,' she said, and she left the pram in the doorway. Her and Ma were in the sitting room drinking cans. So we grabbed a load of empties and took the baby and went out into the corridor between the flats. Mark lined up the cans and we used his football as a bowling ball to knock them over. But the baby kept crying and my ma stuck her head out the door and said the noise was stressing her out and told us to go downstairs.

The lift didn't work and it was real hard carrying the buggy down the stairs. Outside we played a game where you have to try and hit the ball off the corner of the kerb so it bounces into the air, and if you catch it, you get extra points. I've got a deadly throw and I was whipping Mark, but then some lads nicked Mark's ball and started playing football with it, and Mark was scared of them and told me not to say anything. So I didn't cos they were much bigger than us anyway.

The baby was still crying, so we pushed her around for a while but she never stopped. Even when we carried her up the stairs and gave her back to her ma, she cried and cried. My ma and Mark's ma went out that night and we had to stay in listening to the baby cry. That baby never stopped crying.

And then she did.

That's when we left. The next morning, when the baby stopped crying and Ma's friend started crying. Ma grabbed her rucksack and started packing it. Her hands were shaking that morning so it took her ages, even though she was just ramming everything in.

It was real weird cos the baby had been so loud when she cried, but Mark's ma's tears didn't make a sound. Mark was just sitting there chewing a wooden spoon and watching her. I thought that we should help her, but Ma said there was nothing we could do and that the Authorities were coming.

'Sorry,' she said to Mark's ma. Then she grabbed me and we left the flat real quick and ran downstairs.

But I kept thinking, if the Authorities were coming, they could give us a lift back to Gran's, like they said they would when we were camping at the beach. So I stopped running.

It had been raining and the ground was all wet, but it wasn't raining just then. Ma was legging it across the concrete yard, past the slide, and she didn't notice I was still at the bottom of the stairs.

'Ma?'

She stopped and turned. 'What are ye at? Come on!'

'But the Authorities are coming, Ma.'

'Jaysus, I know. Come on, will ye? Now!'

But I didn't move cos I wanted to go back to Gran's.

Ma dropped the rucksack and she legged it back to me.

She grabbed my arm but I still didn't come. 'What are ye doing?' she asked.

'I want to go home,' I said.

Ma gave me her egg-sucking face. 'I'm serious, we have to go.'

'But why, Ma?'

That's when we heard the sirens coming, like a seagull wailing from far away. Ma got all weird. Her eyes got panicky and she cursed. Then she started moving again, pulling me with her.

'Stop it, Ma, you're hurting me.'

A few women had come out of their flats now and were standing on their balconies in their pyjamas. They had babies in one hand and cigarettes in the other.

Ma yanked me again and I yanked back.

When she turned this time, her eyes were so mad that they made me feel real small. Like a worm that Ma had just stepped on or something.

'Do you want to get me arrested?' she asked, but I didn't know what she was talking about. 'If they see us here, they'll take you away from me. You want that?'

'I want to go back to Gran's.'

That's when Ma slapped me. I was so surprised I didn't even cry. I just stared at her. She pointed her finger at me. She was shaking now. I remember noticing her nail polish was peeling off and her nails were all bitten down. Ma used to keep her nails real nice. 'That's enough out of you, ye hear me?' she said, and she yanked my arm again.

When we got to the front of the flats, an ambulance passed us. Ma had her head down and she kept on pulling me. She was still hurting me but I didn't say anything.

We walked. I had to run to keep up with her cos she was walking real fast and pumping her arms like she wanted to punch someone. It started raining but we kept walking. Even when it lashed rain, we didn't stop. We just kept walking. All day. Till the shops started closing, with their shutters half pulled like droopy metal eyelids.

By then Ma wasn't pumping her arms any more. She was holding them close to stop them from shaking. She looked like a snail whose shell has got real heavy from all the rain that's poured on top of it all day. And I didn't have to run to keep up any more neither, which was good cos my feet were all blistered.

We turned at a pub and walked past the backyard where, behind a wire fence, there was a mountain of empty beer bottles and crates. Ma stopped at the next gate. It was painted black, but had this picture of a smiley face spray-painted onto it. It wasn't a happy smiley face, though. It was an evil smiley face with fangs and slanty eyebrows. And when Ma knocked, little bits of the black paint crumbled away. Then I heard the bolt grinding open and a gap appeared, and in the gap were three eyebrows and two massive shoulders.

It was him. Monkey Man.

I jumped behind Ma and pinched her so she knew that I didn't want to be there.

'All right?' he said.

'Hiya,' Ma said.

He was so big that he took up the whole space in the gate. He was leaning against the frame and he looked at Ma like he was counting how many pieces of clothes she was wearing.

Ma flicked her hair back and it whipped me in the face. Then he leaned over and looked at me and said, 'All right?' He lifted his three eyebrows as if he'd just made a joke or something. I hid behind Ma again.

'Listen, just wondering if we could crash here for the night?' she said.

I couldn't believe it. There? With Monkey Man?

"Course,' he said. 'Not a bother, come on in. *Mi casa es su casa* and all that.'

Ma grabbed me and pushed me in front of her. Monkey Man stood back and bowed like Ma was a queen coming home to her castle. But it wasn't a castle. It was a poxy hole.

We stepped into a backyard and there was this huge car that filled most of it. The car looked like it was a hundred years old. It couldn't drive or anything cos it was sitting on blocks. And I don't know how it could have got in there, cos I couldn't see any other gate except the one we'd come through.

Ma had been here before. I could tell by the way she walked straight through the back door and into the kitchen. She threw her bag down and put her sopping wet coat over the back of one of the chairs in the kitchen.

The kitchen had a sink and a fridge and shelves. But there was nothing on them except for a few cups. The bin was so full with wrappers and boxes, though, that there were boxes on the ground too.

'You know where to go. Up the stairs, on the right, after the jacks,' Monkey Man said.

'You're very good, thanks,' Ma said.

'Not a bother,' he said again, and he watched as Ma picked up her rucksack again. He rubbed her arm with his fat paw as she passed. I thought she'd tell him to get off, but she said nothing.

The wallpaper in the hallway was peeling in these long strips that made it look like it had been crying but then its tears dried up cos no one cared. And the steps on the stairs looked like they'd been made from leftover crates from the pub beside the house.

The door to the jacks at the top of the stairs was open. The toilet bowl was yellow and there were empty toilet rolls on the ground beside a broken toilet seat. Then we got to our room.

'Ma!' I said.

'It's grand, isn't it?' she said.

But it wasn't. There was nothing in it. No wardrobe or cushions or duvets. There wasn't even a bed. Just a manky mattress on the floor. There were curtains but they were hung with nails and were only half open. Above the mattress was a mirror with half of the reflective part worn away.

I heard Monkey Man on the stairs. 'Everything all right?' he asked when he got to us.

'Yeah, grand, thanks,' Ma said.

'Good stuff. I'll be downstairs if you want to join me for a drink?'

'Lovely,' Ma said. 'I'll be down in a minute.'

Monkey Man went away again and I just stood there.

'This'll do fine. Just for the night,' Ma said.

'Ma, I don't want to stay here.'

'Don't start,' she said.

'Ma—'

'Would you rather be outside in the rain?' she asked. Then she turned round and looked out the door, down the stairs, and she held her hands together to stop them from shaking. And I knew she didn't care. Not really. What she really wanted was a drink.

'Come on, get those wet things off, you,' she said. And before I could say anything, she was yanking my jacket off and pulling my jumper over my head and then rummaging around in the bottom of the rucksack for my pyjamas. She threw them on the mattress and started unclipping the sleeping bag from the front of the rucksack. By the time she'd laid it out on the mattress, I had my pyjamas on.

'Now . . .' she said. She looked at the door and then back at me. I was just standing there with my hair sopping wet and my feet stinging from the blisters on my toes. And Ma didn't care. She just wanted a can.

And I had to stay on my own in a room with nothing but a manky mattress.

It wasn't fair. I didn't want to be there. Now my hands were shaking too. My whole body was shaking. I was wet and cold and sore, and she didn't care. She was just going to leave me.

I started crying. I couldn't stop. It wasn't just my eyes, neither. My whole body was crying. My throat and my chest and my stomach, and it got louder and louder.

Ma closed her eyes and leaned against the door frame. But that just made me cry harder, till I was all snotty and hiccuping and coughing and I couldn't hardly breathe.

But then she came over. She pulled me onto the mattress and she grabbed a hairbrush from the rucksack and she brushed my hair, and whispered, 'It's all right, love, it's all right.' Then she said, 'I'm sorry, love,' and I think she meant for slapping me when we were outside the flats earlier cos she started wiping my face where she'd hit me. She kept saying it over and over, and kept stroking my face with her shaking hand, till finally I stopped hiccuping and I could breathe normal again. Then she leaned forwards till her forehead was touching mine.

'I'm sorry about today. I just got scared.'

'Why?'

'Cos of that ambulance.'

'Why?'

'Cos first the ambulance comes. Then the coppers follow. And I didn't want to be there when they came.'

But I didn't understand. Cos last time we saw the coppers they said they'd take us to Gran's.

Ma sat up straight and had a long think. Then she said, 'If the coppers saw us, they'd take you away from me.'

'Why?'

'That ambulance? That was coming to take the baby away. But the coppers? They were right behind that ambulance and they would've taken Mark away.'

'Where?'

'Into Care,' Ma said.

'Where's that?'

'It means they take you away from your ma and give you to strangers. Mark's ma will never see him again. He'll be locked up and she won't be allowed to visit.'

'Will they look after him?'

'Not as good as his ma did,' she said.

But I thought of his ma drinking all day and him sitting there chewing a pencil. She wasn't very good at looking after him anyway. I didn't want to think about what strangers would be like. 'What'll they do to him?'

'Depends how wicked the people are that take him,' she said.

And then I felt real bad that we didn't bring him with us cos at least he could have stayed with me, and Ma could have protected him. I hoped he wasn't locked in a room all on his own. And I hoped he knew that he shouldn't draw on the walls in other people's houses.

'We should have taken him with us,' I said.

'Then the coppers would have chased us and they'd have taken him anyway. But they'd have taken *you* as well, and they'd have locked you up and I'd never see you again. And you're the most important thing in the world to me, you know that?'

'But you could come get me, Ma?' I said.

'I couldn't. They'd hide you away, out of the city, where I couldn't find you. And you'd be locked up with people who'd hit you and hurt you and wouldn't feed you.'

'Out by the mountains?'

'Yeah.'

But that didn't make sense either. 'What about the time when the coppers found us on the beach?'

'That time they gave us one chance. That was our only chance. They said if they ever catch you again, though, they'll take you away. And it's not just the coppers, neither. The ambulance people and the social workers, they're all as bad.'

'The Authorities,' I said.

''Zactly,' Ma said.

'I don't want to be taken away, Ma.'

'Then you stick by me and do what I say. And when you see the Authorities, you run, okay?'

But I didn't know what she meant. Did we have to keep running? Couldn't we ever go back to Gran's?

'What about the fishes?' I said, cos it had been months since we'd left Gran's house and summer was over.

'What fish?'

'Everyone's back at school. Who's going to feed the fishes?'

But Ma didn't reply. She just shook her head and looked

out the window. After ages she said, 'Go on, go to sleep now, you're tired,' and she stood up like she was going to leave and I knew she was off to get drunk.

'No, Ma! Don't leave.'

'I'll just be downstairs.'

And I knew I shouldn't say it. I told myself not to. But I did anyway.

'I don't want to be here, Ma. Please? I want to go back to Gran's. The Authorities won't get me there. Gran will save me from them. And I can go back to school and feed the fishes, cos Claire won't give them enough, she doesn't even eat her own Easter eggs, so she'll never feed them. They'll starve!'

I saw Ma's eyes start to sink but I still didn't stop.

'Why can't we just go back to Gran's, Ma? Why can't we go back to normal? I promise I'll hide from the Authorities. I won't even go outside except for school, and Gran walks me there anyway, so she can help me run away from the Authorities, and you wouldn't have to be stressed out.' Then I stopped.

Ma was crying. She was shaking all over. I'd never seen Ma cry before.

I wanted to eat my words back up. I wanted her to stop shaking and stop crying. I wanted to stroke her hair like she stroked mine. But I didn't.

'Ma?' I said.

She was whispering something like, 'What am I doing?'

'Sorry, Ma,' I said.

Ma kept muttering to herself and squeezing her hands together. But then she shook her head like she was shaking the tears away.

She sat and stared at nothing. I didn't say anything. I couldn't. Cos I was looking at her eyes. They'd gone all deep. And I didn't know how to stop them from drowning.

She wiped her face and looked at the door. She made her hands into fists and then shook them out. She sighed. She stood up. 'I'm not going anywhere. I'll just be downstairs, I promise,' she said. And I didn't know what to say to make her stay.

She got me to climb into the sleeping bag and when she kissed me she left salt on my cheek. Then she closed the door.

And even though I didn't want to be there in that room all alone, I fell asleep cos I was dead tired. It was light when I opened my eyes and Ma wasn't beside me.

I crept up to the door. I stuck my head out. It was quiet. I didn't want to go out there. But I had to find Ma.

I went down the stairs real soft. At the bottom, I took a deep breath and peeked around the door into Monkey Man's sitting room. She was there on the couch. Alone.

She was sprawled over it with her arm hanging off the side. Her eyes were open but she wasn't looking at anything.

'Ma?'

She didn't answer. She didn't move.

I ran up to her and knelt beside her. 'Ma?'

I shook her shoulder. I took her hand and I squeezed it. She was cold. But then her eyes swam to mine and she said, 'Never leave me, promise?'

I crawled onto the couch and lifted up her arm and draped it over me. And I don't know if she was asleep or awake cos she kept saying, 'Never leave me.' She said it over and over, but her voice was swimming, just like her eyes.

GLASS TOWER

Ma's not back with the gas or dinner yet. I'm out in the backyard and it's dark now. But it's actually not, cos I brought out fairy lights.

I finished my brick castle the other day. I fished a big plastic sheet out of the canal and used it to cover the ground. Then I got shopping bags and spread them out and hung them to the outside of the walls. So the castle is almost completely waterproof now.

I took the cushions off the couch and brought in a towel as a blanket. But the best part is the fairy lights. I fed them in and out of the holes in the crate that I used for the roof. So now when you lie in the brick castle it's like you're looking at the sky in some exotic place where the stars aren't white, but pink and green and blue. Like Greece or Portugal.

I bet Ma will want to sleep in here. Though it's a little cold. I'd better bring down my duvet.

I'm just going up the stairs when I hear Ma at the front door. I jump back down the steps and sprint through the basement. I try to open the lock but I'm not doing it right cos I'm hurrying too much.

Ma will think it's hilarious when I tell her that Caretaker's been nicking my coins.

When I finally do get it open, I pull too hard and the door comes flying back and I almost fall over. 'Ma, guess what?' I say and I grab the door to steady myself. 'Remember I said I thought the mill was haunted cos–'

But that's as far as I get. A bag of spiders explodes inside me. They race through my spine and up my neck and sink their fangs into my brain.

It's him. Monkey Man. He's here. At our Castle.

'Heya, love,' Ma says and the smell of beer chokes me. She kisses me wetly on the forehead. He's standing behind her with another man.

'Ma, what are they doing here?' I ask.

This is our Castle. Our home. We're safe here. *I'm* safe here. Away from the alleyways and the doorways and the cans and the fighting and the shouting and the hiding and the hunger and the cold and the dark and the scary nights. She's not allowed to bring them in here. She promised.

Monkey Man steps up into our home like he owns the place and stands there looking around. The other guy's real tall but skinny. His clothes are all too big for him. He looks like a scarecrow with glasses and straw hair.

'Ma,' I say, 'what are ya at?'

126

But Ma doesn't bother answering me. She hasn't brought any gas, neither.

Monkey Man whistles like he's making the sound of something falling real fast from the sky. 'Look at this place,' he says. 'It's bleeding massive.'

'Yeah, I know,' Ma says, real proud. 'I call it the Castle.'

I look at her with daggers. I can't believe she's doing this. Why is she showing them our home?

'Ye have this whole gaff to yerself?' he asks.

'Whole gaff,' she says and tries to put her arm around me but I shove her off.

'This way, lads,' she says, and goes straight through the darkness to the kitchen. By the time I get there, they've turned on the set of lights that wraps around the window. The wind-up lamp that Ma got from the Do-gooders is on the table.

'Nice,' Monkey Man says, and he pulls out a chair and sits down. He picks up the lamp and starts winding it. It makes an annoying whirring sound.

Scarecrow wanders around picking stuff up and putting it down again like he's making a list. Ma starts wiping crumbs off the table with her hand as if that's going to suddenly make the place look tidier.

Scarecrow is trying to look out the window, even though it's dark outside. 'What's out there?'

Ma claps her hands and rubs them together and crumbs fall to the floor. 'That's the backyard,' she says and looks at me. 'It's nice when it's sunny. Pretty miserable now, though.'

What is she doing? She's smiling like a total idiot and I want to tell her to shut up.

'Anything out there?' Scarecrow asks.

'Nah, just a couch and old machines and junk like that,' Ma says. Then she points her chin at the kitchen wall. 'Canal runs right by us.'

'Lovely,' he says.

Monkey Man puts the lamp back down and takes a six-pack out of a bag. He hands a beer to Ma but when she tries to take it, he grabs it back. 'Nah, I think you've had enough,' he says and laughs like he's hilarious and hands it out again.

'Stop it, you!' Ma says to him as she takes it and she flicks her hand at his shoulder. She's using her ice-cream voice and it makes me want to puke.

Scarecrow sits down on the other chair and pops open a can. He has all these little holes in his face and it looks like he's trying to grow a beard but he can't cos there are too many holes.

Ma's standing cos we've only two chairs. She's swaying a little and smiling at them.

'So just yerself here then, yeah?' he asks again.

I look at Ma but she doesn't look up. She's scratching her nose with a finger from the same hand she's holding her can with. She nods. Takes another swig. Looks out the kitchen window.

And I don't know why but I just want to say something to make Ma cop on, so I say, 'Caretaker says the mill's haunted, Ma.'

Ma was about to swallow but she coughs and splutters beer all over the place. 'Jaysus,' she says. She wipes her chin with her sleeve. 'Here, lads,' she says, 'do you believe in ghosts?'

They laugh a little. 'Dunno,' Scarecrow says, 'but they believe in me.'

Ma laughs real loud, like this is all hilarious.

'I'll drink to that,' Monkey Man says and he raises his can, and Ma and Scarecrow do too, and they all knock them back. 'Canal runs right by here, ye say?' he says and raises an arm towards the wall.

'That's right,' Ma says.

'So, you going down with the ship?'

'Ha!' Ma says, but she doesn't laugh. 'No, time to move on.'

I freeze. What does she mean, time to move on?

'But I'll drink the place dry and bid it a fond farewell!' Ma nods a few times and they all clink their cans again.

Ma says, 'Getting cold, isn't it?'

Monkey Man opens his arms wide and says, 'Come here and I'll warm ye!'

Ma laughs and tosses her hair back.

'What are you doing, Ma?' I whisper.

Ma looks at me, then out the window. She doesn't say anything. She just takes a gulp from her can. Scarecrow lights a cigarette.

I give her the dirtiest look I can and then I'm off, sprinting up the stairs. Even when the cold air of the sky-bridge hits me, I keep going, up the ladder, right up to the roof.

It's freezing and I'm starving and I can't believe she brought Monkey Man into our home. I just can't believe it.

What did she mean, time to move on? To where?

I squeeze my eyes shut for a second and then pick up the binoculars. The glass apartment has all the lights on and inside it's jammers.

They must be having a party cos there are people all over the sitting room and the kitchen and the balcony, and they are holding silly-shaped glasses that look like they were designed for a game where everyone has to see how long they can hold them without breaking them.

They are all drunk too. Their mouths are wide open and they throw their heads back when they laugh and they wave their hands around like mad, as if they're all having the craziest time. I can't hear them but I imagine they're like Ma, saying stupid things and laughing too loudly. Except they're wearing jewellery that looks like the apartment – bright and sparkling.

There's a man in a black-and-white suit carrying a tray with the stupid-looking glasses on it and the people take the glasses without even looking at him, like the way people give Ma spare change without seeing her.

The guy who owns the apartment takes a glass. He's smiling so wide that I can see all his teeth. The mean-looking lady is beside him. She's like the glasses on the tray, long and skinny and ready to crack. The two of them are standing real close and they're pretending to have the best night ever.

He pulls his hand through his hair and then drops it onto her waist. He slides it around her back. She looks at him and she's smiling. But it's one of those real fake smiles and you can tell that inside she's not smiling. She looks like she hates him about as much as I hate Monkey Man. Her shoulders jerk a tiny bit, as if his hand gives her the creeps. She turns her head away from him and talks to the person beside her. She steps to the side so that his hand drops. He looks at her but she ignores him and keeps on smiling while she nudges further way. Finally he gets the point that she doesn't want to be anywhere near him and leaves her alone.

After a while, she walks away from the people and goes into the kid's room. She turns on the light and everything shines white. Even the wall where the kid drew in red crayon. That's all white again too.

The kid turns over in bed and reaches out a hand. But she must be asleep cos the Glass Woman doesn't go up to her or even say anything. She just turns off the light and leaves. She doesn't go back to the party, though. She disappears for a few seconds and then I see her coming through the door of another bedroom. It has a massive bed with about a hundred pillows on it. She walks up to the window and stares out like she's looking straight at me.

She's got this wild look on her face. There's something about her that reminds me of Ma. Maybe it's the lines on her neck that are pulled so tight they look like the strings on a harp.

But that's not it. It's her eyes. Even though she lives at the top of a glass tower, her eyes look like they're drowning.

It's getting late. And cold. But I don't want to sleep in my room. Not with Monkey Man in my Castle.

I have an idea.

I go back down, into the mill, and straight to our bedroom. I open the window. I grab my duvet and bundle it up and shove it out and let go. It disappears into the night.

I tiptoe downstairs.

At the kitchen door, I peek around. Ma's playing a game where she's balancing a pack of cards half on, half off the edge of the table. The aim is to flip the whole deck over without sending the cards flying.

She's terrible at it. She hits the cards and tries to catch them but the deck scatters across the table. They all laugh.

'Here, give us a shot,' Monkey Man says. 'I'll show you how it's done.'

I hide while the three of them collect up the cards. Next time I look, Monkey Man is balancing the pack on his side of the table.

I drop to my knees. Monkey Man concentrates on the pack. Ma and Scarecrow watch. I crawl through the room as fast as I can. I stay wide. Make no sound.

'Go on,' Ma says. 'Let's see what yer made of!'

I get to the other door when there's a roar. I whip round. The cards are flying everywhere. Scarecrow and Ma are bursting their sides laughing. Monkey Man looks annoyed but he's pretending to laugh. I reach up. Grab the handle. Open the door, slip out, and push it closed behind me. They're still laughing.

I jump up and run through the darkness, over to the couch. I find the duvet hanging off the back of it and I drag it to the brickcastle. I crawl inside, pull the duvet in behind me. I flip over the plastic bag that I use for a door.

All around me the fairy lights blink, like I'm up in the sky, swimming through the stars. It's quiet. No one knows where I am and no one can get into the backyard, except through the kitchen. And as long as there are cans to drink, Ma and the men aren't going anywhere.

I pull the duvet tight around me and burrow my head into the cushions till I'm snug as a bug in a rug. It's just me and my Castle. Now I can sleep.

Then

STEAL AWAY

I hated living in Monkey Man's house.

The days weren't as bad as the nights cos we'd spend them walking all over the city dropping Monkey Man's post off to people's houses. I'm not stupid. I knew what was in the packages. But Ma pretended it was post so I did too.

Real quick, all my blisters turned to leather. They were so hard I could stab them with the tip of a pencil and I wouldn't feel it. I had to get new shoes cos of all the walking and cos my feet kept growing, but Ma didn't mind cos Monkey Man was paying her for delivering his post. She even bought me books to read.

There were always loads of people in Monkey Man's house. I'd see them in the kitchen when we came in, but Ma would take me straight up to the room. She'd stay with me and read me stories till I fell asleep.

Sometimes I'd wake up and she'd be there beside me.

Other times, I'd creep downstairs and there'd be all these people there. Some had mad eyes. And some had sad eyes. And then there were Ma's eyes. Even though Ma said that stuff helped her fly, her eyes were swimming.

One night I woke up. I felt Ma behind me. But I felt something else too. Someone was in the room. I heard breathing.

I opened my eyes. There was a shadow standing by the door. Massive. It was panting.

I couldn't move. I lay there even as it started to come towards me. It bent over. I tried to scream but nothing came out.

The shadow came closer. It had long arms. They dragged off the ground. It lifted one and a hand reached out. In the light from the street I could see its sausage fingers all curled up, about to grab me.

I made a tiny noise but that was all. I tried to kick Ma but I couldn't move. The hand got closer and closer.

Then from downstairs there were voices. Shouting. A door smashing open.

I needed Ma to wake up. I needed her to help me. But I couldn't make a sound.

It was right above me. Dead close. Its breath was so bad it stung my face. Its fat fingers were reaching for my shoulders. It leaned in.

'I know you're awake,' it whispered.

That's when I screamed. I kicked backwards as hard as I could and smacked Ma in the leg. The hand stopped. 'Ma!'

136

The shadow straightened. It was real tall. It had big shoulders that reached up to its neck. It grunted. It stepped back.

'Ma, wake up!' I kicked her and kicked her. She started waking. She made a noise. I kicked her again.

The shadow stood over me for another second. Then it turned and went out of the room.

'What?' she said.

'He was here! He tried to grab me!'

'Who?'

'Monkey Man!' I said.

'Ah, love, it was only a—'

There was a bang downstairs. Then a crash. And then all these voices started shouting.

'Ma, what's going on?'

'Shh!' she said. She sat up and climbed over me. She tiptoed to the door and opened it a little. I heard someone yelping like a kicked dog. But then this low voice like a growl crawled up the stairs.

'That's him, Ma,' I said.

'Shh!' she said again, and she started to go out there.

'No, Ma, don't leave me!' But she was gone.

I was shaking. I could still taste his breath. I could feel it on my neck. I could see his hand reaching for me.

Ma was gone for thirty-seven seconds. Then she was back and the light was on. 'Come on, get up, we're going,' she said.

'Where?' I said. It was still dark outside.

But Ma was ramming everything into the bag so fast that she scared me as much as the shouting. So I pulled a jumper and my coat over my pyjamas and shoved my feet into my new runners. I grabbed my two favourite books off the floor and Ma shoved them into the rucksack too.

'Ready?' Ma said. I nodded. 'Right. Follow me and be real quiet.'

We went onto the stairs. Below us, someone said, 'No, man, you've got it all wrong,' and Ma held her hand up to me when we got to the bottom and she listened.

'Did ye think I was thick?' a man said, and I knew who it was cos the words were curled like he was grinning and growling at the same time.

Ma nodded and we ran, past the room and out the front door.

They didn't see us. But I saw them. A load of men standing in front of a guy who had his back against the wall. That guy saw me. And his eyes were wide and I knew he was as scared as me. Maybe worse. Cos in front of him was Monkey Man. And just as we slipped out Monkey Man turned a bit and I could see he was grinning this big dangerous grin.

That night we went down to the river. We sat there and watched the Lego ships going out to sea, and Ma wrapped the sleeping bag around us. I kept looking back up the river but Ma said that I didn't need to worry any more, Monkey Man wasn't after us.

'They were fighting over some packages of his that went missing,' she said. 'It had nothing to do with us.'

'So why did we run away then?' I asked.

'Cos when he gets mad and he gets an idea into his head, there's no talking to him. It was gonna happen sooner or later.'

'Do we have to go back there, Ma?'

She pulled me onto her lap and she said, 'No, we don't.' And that made me real happy. 'Where do you want to go, love?'

I knew not to talk about Gran's any more. I knew not to stress Ma out. So I said, 'I want to find a castle, Ma. One where it's only you and me. And there's a moat and a drawbridge so no one can get in. It wouldn't have to be fancy or anything. I could be like the princess in the story, the one that lived in the run-down castle.'

'Just you and me?' she said.

'Yeah,' and I meant it. Cos even if Gran wasn't there and even if I couldn't go outside, it'd be enough, as long as no one else could come in. 'And Ma?'

'Yeah?'

'The roof would be really high, so you wouldn't have to fly over the city any more. You could just go up there and feel the wind and you wouldn't be stressed out or anything.'

Ma leaned forwards till her forehead was touching mine. 'That sounds like a grand idea,' she said. 'As long as we're together, we'll be grand.'

'And you'll never let them take me away, Ma, will you?'

'I promise, love.'

'Ma?'

'Yeah?'

'I was real scared tonight.'

'I know, love. But it's all right now. You don't have to be scared, not ever. We'll find a castle, you and me.'

'Promise?'

'I promise.'

She leaned back and pulled me tight against her. 'Now go to sleep. I'll wake you when the sun comes up. Tomorrow's a new day. We'll find a place, you and me, just you wait and see.'

And I believed her.

ROSE

It's afternoon. Monkey Man and Scarecrow are gone and Ma's back at the table with her head in her hands and there are cans lying all over the kitchen. She looks wrecked.

I don't make tea and I don't pick up the cans. I don't even speak to her. I thought when she came down that she'd be real sorry and she'd say she didn't mean to bring them here, that it was only cos she was drunk, and she'd promise never to do it again.

But she doesn't even bother. She just sits there and groans. The kitchen stinks and there's ash on the table but I don't do anything about it. It's her stink. It's her mess.

'I'd murder a cup of tea,' she says.

I don't put on water to boil. There's no gas anyway but I don't tell her that. Instead I pick up the bag that was full of cans last night. Now it just has plastic can holders and a receipt and a few coppers. I turn the bag upside down and everything falls out. I pick up the coins and throw the plastic bag behind me and I'm gone from the kitchen before it floats back down to the floor.

I drop a few coins on the floor of the basement and the rest on the second floor, on top of the dead machines. Then I stand by the window and wait.

It's real dull this morning. It's not raining but the whole world is grey. The clouds are so low I reckon I could stand on the roof on my tippy-toes and touch them. The city looks fed up, like all that's needed is for one person to cry or to breathe too heavily and it'll just melt into the sea.

I think of Caretaker standing on his tippy-toes and looking into the basement and seeing the coins. I wonder if he still thinks it's a ghost or if he realizes it's just me. Part of me thinks he must know, but part of me thinks Caretaker's crazy enough to keep believing in ghosts.

I write my name in the dirt of the window. Then I draw a praying mantis. His arms are held up in front of him like he's praying, but then I draw an insect beneath him and that's the mantis's dinner. He's praying over his dinner before he munches it up.

I breathe on the window and I can see my name in the breath that sticks to it. And the praying mantis looks just like the cranes that are leaning over the city. There's a swarm of cranes out there, crawling over the old buildings and eating their flesh, and the metal frames of new buildings are really the bones of the old ones picked bare.

The cranes look like they are creeping closer and closer.

I turn away from the city and look at the dull room. I wonder if I blow air clouds fast enough can I fill it with fog? I breathe in and out real fast but the breath just disappears.

Then I hear him.

Shuffle, shuffle, shuffle, stop.

He's coming. I don't move. I stay still and wait for him. I hear him climb the stairs. Now he's coming into the room. He looks like a ripped-up bag of rubbish that someone threw out of their car into a bush.

There were only three coins left. He picks those up. He reaches the other machines and sees nothing there and he turns. I'm standing right here but he hasn't hardly noticed me.

'You know it was me,' I say. 'I put the coins down.' But he ignores me. Walks straight past. 'You're crazy,' I say, but I don't think he hears. He goes out of the room and up the stairs.

I go up to the first machine, the one by the door, and I look at the patch in the dust where I put the coin. What's he doing?

I leave the room and follow him up till he reaches the top. But he doesn't go out onto the sky-bridge. He stops and tilts his head up and he stares at something. I come up behind him. There's a trapdoor in the ceiling above the stairs and he's looking at it like there's an answer to a secret up there.

'What are you looking at?' I ask.

He's got a coin in his hand and he's turning it over and over. 'A mistake,' he says. 'See, I thought I'd locked the whole

143

place up. But I didn't think about that.' He points a long, dirty fingernail at the trapdoor. 'She did, though. She did.'

I stare at him. What does he mean, *she*? Does he still believe it was a ghost that put out the coins? I feel kind of sorry for him cos I think he's finally lost it.

'Can you see it? I mean, a ghost or something?'

Caretaker ignores me. He turns and walks out the door onto the sky-bridge and he stops and looks up at the blanket of clouds. I follow. Then I see his face and it snatches my breath away. It's like it holds all the sadness of the night's sky.

I stand beside him and try to think of something nice to say. But I can't. So I say, 'I wonder when it closed down?'

'What?'

'The mill,' I say.

'Forty-seven years ago.'

'You remember when the mill was still open?' I ask.

'Remember? I was here,' he says.

'Really?'

'Caretaker, amn't I?'

'Oh.' I thought that was just a name Ma gave him. I didn't realize he really was the caretaker here. 'How did it work?'

'What do you mean?' Caretaker says.

'The mill and the grain and the work the people did and all that?'

Caretaker looks at me for a minute like he's trying to decide what I'm up to.

'Just wondering,' I say, cos I'd rather listen to him talk than watch his face, all sad and quiet.

He rummages around in his beard for a minute and then says, 'Grain came down the canal in boats. Taken off the boats in bags. If they were wanted for storage, they'd be put in the Silo. If they were wanted for grinding, they came across a conveyor belt that used to be here.' He points to the outside wall of the Silo on the other side of the sky-bridge. Then he draws a line through the sky till he's pointing at the outside wall of the mill. There are matching square holes on both walls. I always wondered what they were for.

He looks at me to see if that's enough, but I don't say anything so he goes on.

'A mill works like one big machine. Each floor is a stage of grinding.' He shuffles back into the mill and goes under the trapdoor and across to the big room on the sixth floor. He points at this massive metal thing that's hanging from the ceiling by a few wires. It's all twisted up and as big as a skip. 'We called that the corkscrew. Grain would come across the conveyor belt from the Silo into the mill, through the ceiling above us here, and then down that chute into the flour bin.

'To start with, the grain got poured into the corkscrew. It got ground up, and would go on down to the next floor and the next and the next. Each floor, more grinding. By the basement, you got flour. Put it in bags. Hauled it out.'

Caretaker nods and turns away from me and goes back out onto the sky-bridge.

'What happened?' I call after him. 'Why'd they close?'

'Times moved on, is all. Wasn't profitable. The men came and closed the place down. That was that.'

The wind blows and catches the rim of his hat but he grabs it just in time. I can feel drops of rain now. I reckon it's going to pour soon.

'So why didn't you go off and be a caretaker somewhere else when the mill closed?' I ask.

Suddenly, I think he's going to cry. He's all slumped over, even more than usual. 'Was my fault. Should never have happened. All my fault.'

'No, it wasn't your fault, Caretaker,' I say. 'You couldn't stop the Authorities from closing this place down. You can't stop them from doing anything. All you can do is hide.'

Caretaker's smile is real watery. 'I'm not hiding, kiddo. I'm just staying, is all. Tied to this place.'

He looks down, below the sky-bridge, at the couch that's covered in a sheet of plastic now that winter's on the way. I can see something in his eyes. It makes my heart stop. He looks sadder than anyone I've ever seen before.

All at once I know something and it makes me feel real guilty.

He's not crazy at all. He has a secret. And it's making him lonely.

'Sorry,' I say, even though I'm not sure what I'm sorry for. But Caretaker looks back up and the sadness is almost gone now, like the wind blew it away.

'Is it a girl, the . . . ?' I stop myself from saying 'ghost' cos I know he doesn't think it's a ghost. He's just remembering something. He doesn't answer, so I say, 'It's just you said *her*.'

He nods. 'She was a girl all right. Near enough to your age. Eyes like a patch of sea when the sun catches it. A million freckles. And a laugh like rain on a tin roof.'

So I was right. The mill does have a story. It just wasn't the one I thought it was.

'Does she have a name?'

He looks down at the couch again and in this tiny voice he says, 'Rose.'

And that's creepy cos I didn't think he really would have a name for her. A name makes her real.

'Who was she, Caretaker?'

But Caretaker doesn't answer.

'You see her?' I ask, just in case he actually is still talking about a ghost.

But now he finally turns and looks real hard at me and he says, 'No. No I don't *see* her,' and the way he says 'see' it's like he's making fun of me. Then he shuffles back inside and begins walking downstairs. As he's disappearing, though, I hear him say something and he's gone before I figure out what it was.

It was, 'And yes, I know it was you.' He means he heard me say that I was the one who put the coins down. That means he heard me call him crazy too.

I follow him to the top of the stairs. But he's gone. Why do I always say the wrong thing?

I'm looking down the staircase but I hear a sound from the big room. I look over and all of a sudden the massive corkscrew thing that hangs in the middle of the room swings. All on its own. I swear. The wind's not strong enough to be doing that but it's still swinging.

I'm not scared of ghosts. I'm not.

But before I know what I'm at, I've turned and legged it across the sky-bridge and up the ladder and onto the roof.

When I reach the wall I check to make sure I'm not being followed.

I'm not.

I look down at the street. It's lunchtime. Red Coat goes into a coffee shop. I grab the binoculars and watch her.

She buys one sandwich and one coffee. She sits down outside, all alone. But she hardly eats anything. Just nibbles. She drinks her coffee, though, and smokes two cigarettes. She doesn't talk to anyone and she doesn't smile.

I look over my shoulder at the ladder. It's okay. Nothing is chasing me.

There's banging coming from the building site across the road. Further down the street I see the two girls that had ribbons in their hair. Their hair is loose and straight now, and they're wearing hairbands to keep it back from their faces.

I wonder who Rose was? And I wonder what Caretaker is really seeing when he's looking at the trapdoor?

But there's something else too. I have that annoying feeling that there's something I should worry about, but I don't know what it is.

I go back to Red Coat, who is looking at something. I focus on her. I think it's a photograph. Then she puts it away and starts walking up the street. I watch her, but really I'm trying to figure out what's annoying me. There's something but I can't find it.

And then I have this flash. I always get this flash. It's like a bit of a memory. I see a blanket. But it's not a blanket, not like Caretaker's blankets. It's something else. It's black.

I don't know what it means, though.

I find the school girls again and follow them crossing the road. They're wearing navy jackets that have pictures on the top-left pocket. Four tiny symbols between the arms of a red cross. I recognize it. I remember it.

I lower the binoculars and try to remember better. A little navy jacket with a red cross on the pocket, hanging on a hook inside Gran's doorway. In her house that was warm and smelled of toast and soap and burning coal. And Gran would help me put the jacket on and give me my pink lunchbox and we'd walk out onto the street and down the road. To school.

'Those girls go to the school with the concrete yard with the pond in the corner! My school!' I almost drop the binoculars over the wall trying to find the girls again. 'That's right near Gran's house!'

But they're gone. I'm about to run to the other side of the roof when, below me, I see two men getting out of a van. They're putting on neon yellow jackets and white plastic hats.

The binoculars crash onto the roof.

The men are standing beside each other and they're

talking. They lean their heads back and they look right up here. I duck down real quick and hide behind the wall.

What are they doing?

I lift myself up a little so I can see over the wall. They have moved. They are right outside the door of the mill. They are trying to open it.

'Please don't,' I whisper.

But Caretaker must have forgotten to lock it when he went out, cos they step inside and disappear. They are in my Castle!

The Authorities are here. They're here. In my home.

I'm sprinting across the roof. It must've been Monkey Man and Scarecrow – they must've told the Authorities about me.

I run as fast as I can down the ladder and across the skybridge and down the stairs of the mill. I want to yell out for Ma, but I know they are in here and they'll hear me.

I have to find her before they do.

Or before they find me.

I turn the corner to the second floor. I see Ma in front of me. She's standing at the door of the bedroom, looking down the stairs. Then she sees me flying towards her. 'The Authorities!' I mouth and I run past her into our bedroom and she closes the door quietly and we both push against it with all our might.

INVASION

I hear their footsteps on the stairs. Their voices sound real big but I can't hardly make out what they're saying. I push hard against the door. So does Ma.

'Any more objections to the planning?'

'It's a one-hundred-and-fifty-million-euro development. That'll soon silence any objections.'

The footsteps are right outside our door. They stop.

'So when are we looking at?'

'Early January, I'd say.'

Stay quiet. Don't shake. Don't breathe too loud.

There's a creak. The handle of the door creeps down. They're trying to get in. I push as hard as I can. Too hard. I slip and my shoes squeak on the floor. They've heard me! They're going to force their way in and they're going to grab me and they're going to take me away, and Ma won't be able to stop them cos they're too strong and she's too hungover.

151

But then the handle springs back.

One of the voices says, 'Locked.'

I think they're starting to move away. I can hear their footsteps and they're talking again, and even though I can't make out what they're saying, their voices are getting further away. They must be looking at the dead machines on this floor.

There is a clanging sound. And a scraping, like something being dragged over the wooden floor. The voices get closer again. I put my hand over my mouth to stop myself from making any noise. They walk past the door and I can hear their footsteps on the stairs and their voices go all muffled and I know they are on the third floor.

Ma breathes out. She turns her back to the door. She bends her knees and leans forwards.

'Ma!' I whisper. 'What do they want?'

There are footsteps on the stairs again. Ma jumps around and pushes against the door and so do I. The voices get closer.

'... structurally unsound. Whole inside will have to go ...'

The footsteps go straight past and down the stairs. I wish there was a statue of the Virgin Mary with a little bowl of holy water at her feet, like the one at Gran's, so I could run over and put my fingers in it and pray that they leave and that they never come back.

I hear a voice from outside the window. I run between our beds and stand on my tippy-toes and put my face against the window. I can't see straight down, not unless I stick my head out. I can only see the stretch by the Silo.

There's nothing there, only a bag filled with empty beer cans. Then I see one of the men and he walks over to the bag and he opens it and looks inside and then he throws it away and I hear it rattle.

Ma's standing beside me and she's got a face like she's in pain. They are her cans. This is her fault. She brought Monkey Man into our Castle. She brought the streets in.

I turn back to the window. The men are standing shoulder to shoulder. They lean their heads back and look up. I jump back.

Ma moves too so that she's in shadow, and she looks down at the men and shakes her head. 'They've seen the kitchen. And the classroom,' she says. 'They know.' She's quiet for a while and I say nothing. Then she curses and says, 'Already?' and she shoves her thumbs into her eyes and shakes her head. After a few seconds, she crosses the room and goes to open the door.

'Don't, Ma!' I say but she opens it real quiet and stands on the stairs. I go up behind her. I can hear their voices. I think they're moving through the basement, so I tiptoe up the stairs as fast and as quiet as I can till I get to the fourth floor, the one with the periscope. I run along the boards by the wall and I make dead sure not to stand on the ones that creak. I crawl across the pipe till I get to the periscope and I stick my ear against it and now I can hear them in the basement and they're talking to each other.

'Obviously has a few squatters. Reckon they're still here?'

'Well, if they are, it won't be for long. Boards are going up after Christmas.'

The voices get muffled and they disappear. I listen a bit longer and then I crawl across the other pipe to the windows. I see the men opening the doors of their van and taking off their plastic hats and their yellow jackets and throwing them inside. They get back into the van and drive away.

'Ma!' I scream and I don't care if I fall through the floorboards and break my neck. I run straight across the room, but I step on a rotted part and it breaks and my foot catches and I fall forwards. 'Ma!' I scream. I smack my elbows on the floor and my foot twists, but I've stopped falling and the board holds. I lift my foot out of the hole real careful and crawl across the dodgy boards to the wall. Then I stop and breathe real heavy. All I want to do is cry.

My foot hurts so I have to limp to the door and when I get there, I hold the railing as I go downstairs.

'Ma!' I'm screaming but I can't find her. She's not in the bedroom and when I go into the kitchen, she's not there neither. I open the back door but she is not in the backyard.

I run into the basement even though my foot stings like mad. And that's where I see her. She's standing in the open doorway.

'Ma! What did they want?'

She stops and turns but I can't really see her face. Her hands are shaking and traffic whizzes past behind her.

'Ma,' I say again. 'What did they want?'

She drops her head and starts biting the skin around her nails.

I think about all the things they said. They said lots of

things. But not about me. They talked about the Castle. Words like 'development' and 'after Christmas'. And they were wearing plastic hats like the people on the building site across the road. 'What were they doing?'

She shakes her head.

'You said "they know". Upstairs. That's what you said. You said "they know". What do they know, Ma?'

'They know there is someone living here,' she says through closed teeth.

'You're the one that brought them here!' I say. 'This was ours! It was safe. You promised, Ma! You promised you'd never bring them in here and you promised I'd never have to go back out there and you promised I wouldn't be scared ever again!'

Her head snaps up. 'Stop it!'

'This is all your fault!' I say.

She takes a few steps towards me and she clenches her fists. 'Enough! There's never an end to it, is there? You'll never leave me be!' she says.

'I hate you!'

The words spill out before I can stop them. And then I see it. The stress that's been growing with every can she opened in the last few weeks.

It's like the octopus tentacles smothering the church. Pulling her down. She's drowning.

She breathes real deep like she's trying to make herself calm and I know she's counting to ten in her head. But even with her hands clenched they are still shaking like mad.

Then she stumbles like she's drunk. But I know she's not drunk right now. She puts a hand out and she leans against the wall. She mumbles. Her shoulders are shaking now too. Her whole body.

'Ma?'

She stands straight and shoves her thumbs into her eyes like she's trying to squeeze them dry. Then she wipes her face and leaves her hands there. 'What am I going to do?' she says from behind her hands but it's real hard to understand her. 'I can't keep doing this. We're out of time.'

I don't know what to say now. I hate her. But I don't. And I don't know how to stop this from happening. Any of it.

Then Ma does something weird. She puts her face right up against the stone. It's like she's whispering to the building. 'Enough! Time to move on,' she says. She slaps the wall with an open hand. Then she turns and flops back against it. She looks at me. And there's no anger left in her eyes. They're empty.

'I can't. It's too hard,' she says.

She's crying. Ma's crying. And she doesn't even brush the tears away.

'It's all right, Ma,' I say.

'No. It's not,' she says. 'Cos no matter what I do, I can't stop it from happening.'

I think she means that she can't stop the Authorities from coming. But maybe she means she can't stop herself from drowning.

A tear drips off her chin and splashes on the floor. She

reaches out her hand to me but then she stops, like she changed her mind.

She's drowning and I can't save her.

She turns her head and looks out at the traffic and the people. But I know what she's really looking for. The same thing she always looks for when her eyes go that deep.

'Please, Ma, don't do it,' I say.

Ma takes a deep breath. She looks straight at me. Tries to smile. But she can't. A tear rolls down her face and drains away her smile like a sandcastle washed away by waves.

She sighs. She turns. She walks right out the door. And I'm standing and staring and my heart is tearing. 'Ma!'

But Ma doesn't hear me any more. She doesn't care.

I know where she's going. To knock on the black rusted gate with the evil smiley face.

And I can't stop her.

Then

A CARDBOARD CASTLE

The morning after we left Monkey Man's house and slept by the river, we started walking again. I kept asking Ma where we were going and if we were going to find a castle. She said castles weren't easy to find and that it might take a few days.

Ma's hands were shaking but her eyes were as clear as the air that morning, so I wasn't worried.

We walked for hours and hours searching for a castle. We must have looked weird, with Ma carrying her rucksack and me still in my pyjama bottoms, cos that was the first time I noticed the way some people can look everywhere except at you.

Like this one woman walking with her kid. I saw her notice us from down the street, cos she grabbed her kid's hand and dragged him to the other side of the path. When they got close, the kid stared at me. But the ma looked straight ahead. Then the kid said, 'Mummy, why is that girl wearing pyjamas?' But the ma didn't answer. Instead she walked faster till they were past us. And the whole time her eyes looked straight ahead.

That's the thing. People can see you coming from a mile off. You're only invisible up close.

We got to this crossroads that had a sign for the zoo on one side and the train station on the other and loads of traffic zooming past. Ma turned towards the train station.

At the entrance to the station there was a coffee shop, and Ma went straight up to the counter and took a load of napkins and turned and walked out. Then we went into the ladies' jacks. There were people queueing but Ma went straight to the sinks and filled one with water. She took off her T-shirt and started washing everywhere, even under her arms.

'Ma,' I said. 'Everyone's staring.'

There was this woman that was wearing a posh black-and-white skirt and matching jacket. She was watching Ma with this look on her face like she'd just drunk sour milk.

'What are ye gawping at?' Ma said and the woman looked away.

Ma dried herself with the napkins and chucked them in the bin. Then she took out her hairbrush and brushed her hair. Then it was my turn.

I changed into real clothes. Then Ma wet a napkin and rubbed my face so hard it hurt. 'Ow, Ma!'

'Don't be such a whinge,' she said, but she was laughing.

This other woman came in to the jacks and when she saw

me, she shook her head. 'What are you looking at?' I said, and the woman tutted. Ma winked at me.

I brushed my teeth and then Ma said, 'Do you need to use the jacks?'

'Yeah.'

'Right,' Ma said, and when the toilet door opened, she shoved me in front of the tutting woman. 'Sorry,' Ma said. 'We were here first.'

When I got out, the woman was gone. But then a minute later the security guard came in. 'Sorry, yis can't be in here,' he said.

'Neither can you, it's the ladies' jacks,' Ma said. 'We're leaving anyway.'

When we left the train station we went back to the signposts. Behind us was a pub and across the road was the archway that you go under to get into the park, the big one that has the fields and the trees in it. The zoo is just up the road.

'Wait here,' Ma said and she went in under the archway. When she came back a while later, she didn't have the rucksack. 'Right,' she said. 'Hungry?'

'Where's the rucksack?' I said.

'I stashed it. Come on.'

She grabbed my hand and we went into the pub. We sat down at a table that was right beside the door. When the woman came over, Ma said, 'Give us a menu.' But a second later, she said, 'Please.'

We ordered the best food ever. Loads of egg mayo and ham sandwiches, and soup and Coke. For dessert I had a massive slice of chocolate cake with the icing all melted and gooey. Ma ordered the same but she only ate the soup. She had a few pints as well, though.

When we finished, Ma said, 'Go across the road, under the archway and to the left. Wait for me there.'

'Why?'

'Just do it.'

I did. I waited ages. So long that I was about to go back for Ma when she came flying around the archway. 'Come on,' she said and she grabbed my hand and started legging it towards the trees.

'Ma, stop, I'm too full of food!'

'Run!' she said, so I legged it, even though the chocolate cake was stuck in my throat.

When we got into the trees we ran along a trail. It was all overgrown and bursting with green. There was loads of cardboard everywhere cos loads of people had slept there. After a while, we slowed down.

'You didn't pay, Ma, did you? For the food?'

'I did!' she said in this voice like she was real offended. 'I just didn't leave a tip.'

'You're such a liar,' I said. Ma didn't reply to that.

We came up to this one guy who was just standing there, staring at nothing. Ma's rucksack was beside him.

'Thanks,' she said when she picked it up and she handed him the bread rolls that had been in the basket when the woman brought us our soup. He took them but he didn't say anything.

He had tied a piece of plastic into the branches above him to keep the rain off, and below were a few sleeping bags. He must've been living there for a while.

'Coppers been around at all?' Ma asked, and he shook his head real slow.

We went on through the trees, and I was thinking of the forest with the eyes that followed the princess, when we came up to this big old shed. It was tall and wide, but it didn't even have a proper roof on it any more. Just wooden beams and pieces of slates, but there were loads of holes in it. I stared at Ma.

'We're just resting here, love. Let me sit down for a minute, will ye?' she said and she went inside.

'Ah, Ma, it's a shed!' I said, cos I knew that meant we were going to sleep in there.

'More like a barn,' Ma called out. I followed her inside and watched her. She went to say something but then she stopped, like she changed her mind, and instead she said, 'One night, I swear on me own grave, just for tonight. The weather is grand, we'll sleep here and find a place tomorrow. Deal?'

I looked around at the ring of black stones where someone had lit a fire before, and then up at the holes in the roof.

'Just for tonight,' she said again.

'Fine,' I said. 'But you have to help me make it better.'

Ma looked at me and shoved her hands in her pockets, but her eyes were smiling. So I ran out into the trees and grabbed a load of cardboard boxes and brought them back and threw them into the middle of the shed.

'Come on!' I said.

Ma laughed and shook her head but she came with me and together we brought back loads of cardboard boxes and piled them as high as our heads.

'Now what?' she asked.

'Now we build a castle,' I said.

I took down the first box and I opened it out and then started folding it up into a tube shape. Ma watched me do it a few times and then she said, 'Wait here, I'll be back.'

And she ran off before I could say anything, so I just kept opening out the cardboard boxes and folding them into tube shapes, and hoping she'd come back. She was gone ages. But then she did come back. With a six-pack and two rolls of tape and a packet of cigarettes.

I started taping the boxes so they'd keep their tube shape, and then we put one tube beside another and taped them together so we had a long tube.

We built loads of tubes and stuck them together, and we made corners as well, so in the end we had this deadly maze with corridors and corners and side rooms, and you could crawl through it and get lost in it for days.

Then we made towers and we put them on top of the maze. With the last of the cardboard, I built a wall around the whole thing.

'What's that for?' Ma asked.

'That's to keep the intruders out. We don't have a moat but the wall's real high so they can't climb over it,' I said.

And Ma sat down and laughed as she drank her last can.

And when I was finished building the wall, I sat down beside her and ate the left-over sandwiches that Ma had taken from the pub. There was cake too and it was real good, even though the icing was gloopy instead of melty.

'We'll find our own castle, though, won't we, Ma?'

'We will,' she said.

'Tomorrow?'

'Yeah, love. Tomorrow.'

Ma crushed her last can and threw it away. Then she crawled into the middle of the maze with me and told me a story about a princess stuck in a castle who couldn't leave till a prince came and rescued her. But I said it was stupid to wait for a prince to come rescue you when you could just find the secret way out, cos there's always a secret way out from a castle.

And when I fell asleep, I knew Ma would be right there beside me and that we'd be safe in our castle.

THE STARS GO OUT

I'm lying in bed in our room. I brought the duvet and the lights back in from my brick castle. Ma's not home yet. I wish she'd come back.

It's real quiet. The office workers are all gone home and the cars have left the city and the seagulls are gone to sleep. There's a scratching sound coming from the stairway but it's just a rat. Sometimes in the morning you find them dead in a corner somewhere, with their guts all hanging out. That's the cats. You don't hear the cats, though, cos they're too smart.

The rats eat the food from the skip and the cats eat the rats. Nothing eats the cats, though. They're king of the Castle. They just come and go, over the walls and through the gaps. No one even cares what they do. No one is looking for them.

The fairy lights above my bed twinkle. I'm telling myself a story about a princess that gets kidnapped and then escapes.

Right now, she's fighting her way through an enchanted forest but there are evil men chasing her. I wonder, are enchanted forests like castles, do they have a secret escape route?

Three loud knocks fold the silence in half. I jump up. Yellow Jackets again? But they said, 'Boards are going up after Christmas.' And it's not Christmas yet.

I hear them again. Two knocks, then a pause, then a third. It's okay. That's Ma's knock. She's back.

I run downstairs.

At the door I run my hand up the side till I find the key that's on the hook. When I open the door Ma's standing there, crouched over.

Her hands aren't shaking any more.

'Heya, love,' she says. But she says it like she's underwater and the words are real heavy and they're pulling her down.

'Ma?'

'You're here,' she says, and smiles as if she thought I'd be gone or something. 'Came back, didn't I? Me and you against the world, eh?' she says.

Then she starts fumbling around in her pocket like she's making sure whatever's in there is still safe. There's a little bulge in her jeans and I know what that means. She steps inside and wobbles off towards the kitchen.

I don't follow her. I just lock the door and go back up the stairs to bed. I turn off the stars and stare at the darkness. I pull the duvet tight around me. I lift it over my head.

She promised she'd never go back there. But she broke her promise.

PART

THREE

MAKE-BELIEVE

I'm drawing on the walls of the second floor. Outside, the cranes have munched away a whole office block like it was never even there. I bet there were people inside and they didn't get out in time and the cranes munched them up too.

There are more cranes these days. I can see thirteen just from this window. They're all creeping closer, as if there's a building that's bleeding and they can smell it and they are coming to devour it.

I've painted thirteen praying mantises on the wall, just like outside. Except in my drawing, people aren't sitting around drinking coffee. They are all running away screaming, cos the mantises are tearing apart the buildings and are coming for them too.

I hear something.

I turn and look at the dead machines. There's nothing there.

I've painted loads of destroyed buildings and now I'm going

to add some trees growing out of the rubble. Then I'll paint new buildings, but there'll be ivy crawling up the outside walls, smothering them.

There it is again. The sound. Like someone moving real quiet through the room. I turn again but I can't see anything. Just the machines and lots of dust drifting. Even as I'm looking, though, I hear it again.

I stand dead still. It's probably just wind or something. I turn back to the wall, but as I do I spot something.

I turn my head from one side to the other and now I see it. It's the air. The dust in the air. It's moving.

I don't know how to explain it. The dust isn't drifting around like it usually does. It looks like it's flowing through the room. I pretend to start painting again but really I'm watching from the corner of my eye. And I can see it's not flowing everywhere. In some areas it's not moving at all.

I whip my head round but now I can't see it any more. I move up to the closest machine, real careful, and walk all around it.

There's something wrong. I can't figure it out. I try to look at the air but it's real hard, cos how do you watch air? Instead I watch the space above the machine

Then I get it. I know what it is.

In some areas the dust is flowing but in other areas there *is* no dust. Close to the machine, the air above looks empty, like the dust avoids it.

And now it's moving! The empty space! It's drifting away from the machine!

I take a step backwards. Then another. All the way till I'm

beside a pillar. I duck behind it, hide my body so it's just my head poking out. I watch.

I see it. The dust is parting and the empty space is moving through the room. It's going from one machine to the next.

I drop to the floor. Squeeze my eyes shut. Take a deep breath.

Then I open them. I scramble around the pillar. Crawl on my hands and knees till I reach the next. I lift myself up a little and squint.

I can't see it now. I think it's moved to the machine by the door.

I push myself up and run fast around the pillar and stand with my back pressed flat against the next. I peer around.

It's there. By the door. Now it's rushing out of the room. I sprint after it.

I think it's turning up the stairs but I can't be sure. Blood rushes from my head to my stomach. I leg it up the stairs two at a time. At the top I swear I see an empty space in front of me. Then it disappears. Right beneath the trapdoor into the ceiling. The one that holds Caretaker's secret.

I'm panting and shaking and seeing stars. But I don't see anything else. Not any more. It's gone.

After ages I turn to go downstairs. Maybe I should tell Caretaker.

Or maybe not.

Cos it might upset him. Or scare him. But it doesn't scare me. Cos I'm not afraid of ghosts. I'm not.

I turn back.

'What's up there, Rose?' I whisper to the trapdoor.

Then I have an idea.

I run down to the classroom, grab a chair and bring it back up. I put it in the corner, beneath the trapdoor, and climb up. But I'm still not tall enough to reach it. So I go down to the backyard and grab some bricks and run up with them. I kick the chair out of the way and stack some bricks. Then I run down and up and down and up, and I keep on going until I've brought up about a million bricks and I've built a big box platform. I put the chair on top of that. I climb up on the box. Then up on the chair. Now I'm so high my head touches the trapdoor and I have to bend over.

I push it. It doesn't budge. I smack it real hard. It still doesn't move. But then I whack it and it flies open and dust falls into my mouth. The chair wobbles and I almost topple off, over the bricks and down the stairs. I grab the edge of the trapdoor and hold tight. When I'm sure I'm safe, I take a deep breath and go up on my tippy-toes.

I'm looking into the gap between the ceiling and the roof. It's like the attic in Gran's, though I don't think mills have attics. There's light coming from somewhere. Perhaps it's the square hole in the wall of the mill that's above the sky-bridge, where Caretaker says the conveyor belt came in. I pull myself up into the attic. I have to crouch. I blink a few times. I crawl towards the sunlight coming in through the hole in the wall, but I'm being real careful cos I can hardly see anything.

When I get close to the light, I see it. The conveyor belt. It doesn't run through the air over the sky-bridge any more but the part in the attic is still here. It's hard but rubbery.

I stick my head out of the square hole into the wind. The sky-bridge is below me and then nothing, all the way to the couch.

I turn round and crawl past the trapdoor. There's a shiny silver chute ahead of me. I know what this is. It's how the grain from the conveyor belt came into the mill. It slid through this chute into the big bin on the sixth floor that has old bags of flour in it.

'Why did Caretaker look so sad when he talked about you, Rose?' I whisper to the attic. 'What happened?'

I touch the inside of the chute. It's smooth and cold and made of metal. I reckon it would make a pretty good slide.

I think of Ma's mates daring her to break into the church. 'You dare me to slide down it, Rose?'

I pretend that I hear a laugh, like rain hitting a tin roof, and in the darkness I can almost see eyes glinting like sunlight catching a patch of sea.

I laugh too. 'Whoop, whoop, hurray! See you another day!' I say and I put my legs through the metal chute and push off, and it's so smooth it's like falling through water and the whole world becomes a tin can, and I whoosh down and suddenly I fly out into the light and I plop onto the old bags of flour.

I laugh real loud and I can hear it bounce through the metal chute. 'Your turn, Rose!' I call up into the chute. 'Don't be scared – the machines aren't grinding any more!'

But I hear the floorboards beneath the bin. They rattle

and creak. I sit up and look over the side. The boards are real rotted up here and I'm scared that the whole floor will collapse.

In the middle of the room the massive metal thing sways and I realize that it actually does look like a corkscrew, like Caretaker said. Back then, when the mill was open, I bet the corkscrew was standing in the middle of the room, all safe and secure, but now it dangles off the ceiling by a few metal threads like it's a bullet waiting to be fired.

I lift myself out of the bin real careful and it takes me ages to crawl across the floor cos there are more holes than floor. When I get to the doorway I stand up and look at the chute. I imagine a girl my age coming flying out of it and bouncing into the flour bags, and the flour rising in a big cloud and filling up the whole room.

But there's really no one here. All there is, is a bit of dust and flour floating in the air.

Then

YELLOW JACKETS AND BUSYBODIES

Ma promised we'd only stay one night sleeping in the shed in the park. She didn't keep her promise.

The next day we stashed the rucksack in a bush behind the shed and we went off looking for a castle. As soon as we stepped outside the park, though, we saw two coppers coming up the street. Across the road, the woman from the pub came outside.

Ma cursed and grabbed my hand, and we ducked behind the pillar of the archway and waited. After a while, Ma said, 'Right', and she pulled me back through the arch. The coppers were gone and so was the woman from the pub.

Ma's hands were already shaking, and the more we walked, the more they shook.

'Ma,' I said, 'What about that? That could be our castle.'

I pointed to this building that was so new, it looked like it was wrapped in blue plastic. I was only messing but Ma said, 'Don't be bleeding stupid.' She started walking even faster.

By the time Ma's eyes started to sink, her arms were pumping. We'd reached the street in the middle of the city that's packed with people, the one where cars aren't allowed to drive. I didn't want a castle there. And I didn't think there'd be one anyway. It was too crowded.

'Ma, do you think we'll find a castle today?'

Ma didn't answer. She was looking at this van that was parked in a side street. It looked like a chipper van, only they weren't selling chips. They were selling clothes. Ma was biting her nails, even though she had no nails left to bite.

'See them?' she said. She pointed to some people that were wearing neon yellow vests, standing around the van.

'Yeah?'

'Don't ever go near them. Bleeding Do-gooders. They work with the coppers, you know?'

I didn't know. But Ma looked stressed and I knew not to say anything.

'Stay here a minute,' she said.

Ma went over to the Do-gooders and started talking to them. After a bit they handed her a load of stuff and she walked away. She hadn't paid, but they didn't seem to care. Ma came marching up to me and right past me. She didn't even stop. I had to run through a crowd of people to catch up.

'Ma, what's that?'

'New clothes. You can throw away your dirty ones.'

I didn't want to throw them away. They only needed to be cleaned.

'My runners too?'

'No, ye eejit,' she said.

'Ma, you didn't pay for them.'

'No,' she said.

'Why?'

'Cos they're free.'

'Why?'

'Cos that's what they do. Give out clothes and soup, and take information back to the coppers. They're all in it together, the coppers and the ambulance people and the Do-gooders.'

'And the social workers,' I reminded her.

''Zactly,' Ma said. 'All them Yellow Jackets and busybodies. So don't you go near any of them, ye hear?'

'Yeah,' I said.

We kept walking up the street and I kept a lookout for the Authorities.

'Ma, are we going to find our castle now?'

'Jaysus, enough!' she said.

I nodded and I said nothing for ages. Loads of times I wanted to ask where we were going but I didn't. Not even after lunch when we just got up and started walking again.

By the time it started getting late, though, I was worried cos I didn't want to sleep in the park again. Ma had promised. So I said, 'Are we sleeping in our castle tonight?'

That's when Ma spun round and I saw that her eyes had sunk to the bottom of her head. 'I said enough! Just stop! Going on all day at me, stressing me out!'

It wasn't fair. It was only the third time I'd asked in the whole day. But Ma was looking at me the same way as she had the last time she slapped me. Maybe the only reason why she didn't slap me again was cos her hands were full of clothes. So I said nothing. I just kept walking. But then we came up to the black rusted gate. With the evil smiley face. And my heart fell into my runners.

'Ma!' I said.

She knocked real loud. The bolt grinded back and forth. I hid behind her. A second later I heard his voice.

'Look what the cat dragged in!'

I didn't look at Monkey Man. I stayed hidden. But his head appeared around Ma's shoulder. 'And your precious daughter too.' I closed my eyes so I couldn't see him.

'Just sort me out,' Ma said.

'Not coming in then?'

'No. Thanks.'

'Where ye staying?' Monkey Man asked.

'A mate's,' she said.

There was silence for a while and then he said, 'Suit yerself. What'll it be?'

When Monkey Man disappeared for a minute, I stood back from Ma and made her look at me.

'Ma? Please? I don't want to stay here.'

'We're not. I'm just collecting something.'

And at least she wasn't lying cos a few seconds after Monkey Man came back, we were walking again. This time I didn't care that we were going back to the shed in the trees. Anything was better than staying there.

CHRISTMAS IN THE CASTLE

It's Christmas Day. I'm sitting outside the basement in Caretaker's room. I don't even smell him any more. I've got three blankets wrapped around me. Caretaker went to the building where the Do-gooders give out food and he brought me back a mince pie. I haven't touched it, though, cos I don't think mince in pie sounds very nice. Gran used to make burgers with mince and they were real good. But she never used it for pie. She'd use apples or rhubarb or something.

'I like your hat,' I say.

Caretaker's wearing a Santa hat over a black wool one.

'It brings out my eyes,' he says. 'It was a present from the centre. Bunch of down-and-outs and junkies wearing Santa hats. Now there's a sight worth seeing,' he says and fixes his sunglasses with the one lens and then he starts rummaging around under the blankets.

'Got you a present,' he says.

'You did?' I say and I'm excited, but I feel a bit bad too cos I don't have a present for him.

He holds it out to me and it's wrapped in brown paper and I know it's a book cos I can feel it. I rip the paper off. On the cover is a fireplace with stockings hanging from it. The fire's blazing and it looks real warm. It reminds me of Gran's house at Christmas.

I had a stocking too and it had my name on it. There weren't any hooks for hanging it to the fireplace, but on Christmas morning it'd be lying against the wall in the sitting room and it'd be so full that it'd stand up all by itself.

I open the book and flick to the end. The last picture is of a mountain. It's covered in snow. Above the mountain there are all these green lights in the sky.

'Hey, Caretaker, what's this?' I ask and I hold up the book and point at the lights in the sky in the picture.

'Them's the Northern Lights. The aurora borealis. Made by the Hidden Folk who live at the North Pole and spread magic over the world at Christmas.'

I trace my finger over the lights and I imagine being there and watching them.

'You ever been up to the North Pole?' I ask him.

'Yeah,' he says.

'What's it like?'

'Cold. Beautiful.'

'Why were you there?' I ask.

'Got lost.'

'What did you do?'

'Tried to get home. Took me a while, mind you. And by the time I got back, everything'd changed.'

And I know he's just telling stories but I'd love to see them. The Northern Lights. And trudge through snow so deep I'd sink up to my chin. 'I'm going to go there some day when I'm grown up and the Authorities aren't after me any more.'

'Why don't you just go now?'

'Can't,' I say. I lift the mince pie and I try to make myself take a bite. But all I can think about is slithery pink worms of raw meat. Is the mince in the pie cooked? It must be.

'Why not?'

I look at him for a second before I remember what we're talking about. Going to the North Pole. 'Cos. I can't. Ma needs me. I don't leave her and she doesn't leave me. That's the deal. Anyway, she can't fight off the Authorities on her own.'

Maybe the pie will taste like a burger, with ketchup and all. I'm about to take a bite when Caretaker says, 'What about next year? Where are you going to spend Christmas?'

'Here.'

'No, you're not,' he says.

The mince pie is touching my lip. 'Why?'

'Cos the times are a changing, kiddo. Time to move on.'

I drop the mince pie onto my lap. 'Why does everyone keep saying that?'

Caretaker doesn't answer. Instead he says, 'Where's your ma?'

'Upstairs. In bed, I think.'

'Not doing so well, ha?'

'She's stressed out,' I whisper.

'Why's that?'

'The Authorities,' I say to the mince pie.

'Huh?'

'The men in the yellow jackets,' I say a little louder. 'They came in here. They stressed Ma out.'

'And they'll be back.'

I look up. Someone is walking along the street above us. They stop by Caretaker's books. It's Short Guy. I nearly didn't know it was him cos he doesn't look that short when he's not standing beside Red Coat. He's scanning the books. Actually, he's staring at one book.

Caretaker stands up and watches him, which is weird cos he never speaks to the book buyers. He never talks to anyone but me and Ma.

'Forty-three days,' Caretaker says.

This makes Short Guy look down at him. I look at Caretaker too cos I don't know what he's going on about.

'That's how many days you've stopped here and stared at *Ulysses*,' Caretaker says. 'Didn't think you'd come today, though.'

Short Guy doesn't say anything for ages and when he does, he sounds nothing like I thought he would. He sounds real serious. And he's not from the city cos his accent's real weird.

'Forty-five,' Short Guy says. 'It's been forty-five days.' He

186

crouches down and picks up *Ulysses* and turns it over. He doesn't read the back or anything, just bounces it in his hand like he's trying to guess how heavy it is.

'We used to pass here every day. We'd joke that the day *Ulysses* was gone would be the day we'd leave the city and start a new life . . . Somewhere. Anywhere. It didn't matter.' He stops bouncing the book. Him and Caretaker look at each other. 'We never said where we'd go. But I believed we would. Some day. You know?' Then he looks down the street like he's watching her walk away.

'Why can't you still go?' I say before I remember I'm not supposed to speak to anyone from outside. But it's okay cos he doesn't hear me. He's too busy thinking.

Caretaker heard me, though, cos he waits till Short Guy turns back to us and then he says,

'Isn't there still a way?'

Short Guy shakes his head. He's almost whispering when he says, 'She won't forgive me.' He looks at Caretaker, like Caretaker might forgive him instead.

I wonder what he did that was so bad. Caretaker doesn't ask him, though. All he says is, 'Time to move on?'

But Short Guy doesn't reply. He just shakes his head like he doesn't agree and puts the book back down.

'Take it,' Caretaker says. He means *Ulysses*.

Short Guy doesn't. Instead he picks up another book. He doesn't even bother to read the title. He stands up and roots around in his pocket and throws twenty quid in Caretaker's cup.

'Merry Christmas,' he says. He nods at Caretaker. Then leaves.

We both watch him till he's gone. After a while, Caretaker lies back down and pulls a blanket around him.

'She should forgive him,' I say.

'Why?'

'Cos he looks real sorry,' I say.

'Maybe what he did was very bad.'

'Yeah. But she should still forgive him anyway.'

'Maybe she's happier without him,' Caretaker says.

'She's not. She's real sad. She never laughs any more.'

He peels back the blanket from his chin so he can see me. He's wondering how I know that. He's waiting for me to tell him but I don't. He doesn't ask though. He says, 'Maybe what he did was unforgivable.'

I think about that for a while. I don't know if anything is unforgivable. Not if you're real sorry. I mean, I don't think he killed anyone or anything like that. Cos I think he's probably real nice.

Caretaker snuggles back under his blankets again. I pick up the mince pie. It smells okay. I go to take a bite. But then I remember what we were talking about before Short Guy arrived.

'Caretaker?'

'Mmm?'

'What's a one-hundred-and-fifty-million-euro development?'

He opens his eye and squints at me. 'That's one big, shiny digital future and there ain't no escaping it.'

I don't know what that means but I have an idea. The cranes. The plastic-wrapped buildings with the perfect windows and perfect corners. 'But it's our Castle,' I say.

'As the old saying goes, "One man's castle is another man's hundred-and-fifty-million-euro development",' he says. Then he says, 'You should forgive her.'

'Who?'

But he doesn't tell me. Just says, 'You have to move on.'

'Where? We've nowhere to go,' I whisper.

'Out there. Anywhere. The ether. The big bad beyond.'

'You don't understand,' I say.

'Understand? Course I do. Been here fifty years, haven't I?' He sits up straight and looks at me so hard, it's like he's trying to see through me. 'People get stuck. But time moves on. And now they're coming to get us.'

Then his eye goes real wide. He tilts his head back and raises a fist. He shakes it at the city. 'The future will not be ignored. The mill and her ghosts are crumbling into the canal. She'll take us all with her if we can't escape first.'

He stares at the sky for ages. His sunglasses slip a little and I nearly see his other eye. But he pushes them back up before I get to see it. Then he settles back down again and sighs. He notices my mince pie. 'Not eating that?'

I hand it to him. He lifts it to his mouth but he looks at me. 'You've got to move on,' he says 'Let all this go. Easier said than done, I know.' He nods, over and over again. 'You'd think I'd take my own advice.'

Then he pops the pie in his mouth, the whole thing at once, and when he swallows, he doesn't even bother brushing the crumbs off him. He just pulls his hat down and lies back. 'But not today,' he mumbles. 'That's a problem for the New Year. Merry Christmas, kiddo.'

I run up to our room. Ma's there, on the bed. I push in beside her and pull her arm over me.

'Happy Christmas, Ma,' I say.

She starts talking like she's underwater. 'So small. So cold. My fault. But I came back.'

'Don't worry, Ma. The Castle is safe.'

'Never leave me,' she says. 'I'll always come back.'

'I won't let them take it, Ma.'

'I promise,' she says. But she's just saying words. They don't mean anything.

'We'll fight them, Ma. If they come back. We'll scare them away. So you don't need to be stressed out.' I turn to look at her. Her eyes are open. But they don't see.

'I always come back, don't I, love?' she says.

'Yeah,' I say.

But coming back's not the same as being here.

I'm on the roof. The city's real weird on Christmas Day. Like it's dead. The cranes looking like mantises praying for Christmas to end so they can start eating again.

It's cold and it's clear and there's a little bit of snow on the top of the mountains. It looks like the sun is trying to break through the clouds but it has no energy left, it's too weak, and it has decided to give up and go back to bed.

The streets are empty. No one is walking or working or buying coffee. The green boat has lights around the windows and they flash red and yellow. Inside, the woman has the baby strapped to her front and she's chatting away as she cooks. Behind her is an old woman sitting on a couch. I think it's Boat Woman's ma cos they look like each other. Both of them have big noses and hardly any chin at all.

Boat Woman walks outside. The swans are there. There's only the ma and dad swan now, and one baby. Except the baby's as big as them and all its feathers are white. Maybe the other two babies left cos they're too grown up to stay with their ma and dad. Maybe the last baby isn't as brave as the others yet.

Boat Woman throws pieces of food to the swans and they snap it up. Seagulls swoop down too and they dart in and out of the swans. Boat Woman stands back and shoos them away. I think she's scared they'll grab her baby like they grabbed those two other baby swans a while ago.

I wonder where they'd take a human baby if they did snatch it. Maybe they'd fly it up to the mountains.

And Boat Woman would feel real guilty that she let the seagulls take her baby away. And she'd spend years trying to find it.

But that won't happen. Cos her baby's strapped on real tight.

I look up at the glass apartment. The man and woman are

there. She looks like a glass angel in a pink dress and she's carrying a turkey to the white table. He stands and picks up a knife and spends ages cutting pieces of turkey that are all the exact same size. She puts a napkin on her lap and smoothes it out, over and over again.

Finally they start eating. At least he does, shoving huge pieces of meat into his mouth. She spends her time cutting it into tiny pieces and then chewing each piece for an hour.

There's a big green tree in the corner. There are all these empty boxes and presents on the floor. I bet you could build a cardboard castle big enough to fill the whole room with them. But I don't think Glass Woman would like that very much. Anyway, the kid's not trying to build anything. She's just watching TV. She's not even playing with the new toys.

I wanted to ask Ma for a hairband for my Christmas present. Like the girls from my old school wear. But there was no point. I should have just asked for cardboard boxes. She'd have been able to get them.

I drop the binoculars and turn around. The clock on the church looks like a full yellow moon. I walk to the other side again and I lift the binoculars and I look for a concrete yard with a pond in the corner, somewhere out there in the direction that the girls walk every day.

Is Gran having turkey and ham and potatoes with gravy?

I bet she is. That's what we used to have. There'd be so much turkey that we'd be having it in sandwiches for days after.

I walk back to the canal side again. There's smoke coming

out the chimney of the green boat. Inside, Boat Woman and her ma are chatting and eating. The baby is asleep on the couch beside the gran.

I wonder, was it like that in my gran's house when I was a baby? I wonder, did Ma and Gran used to chat and laugh. Before it went bad.

But I see Gran's face, the day we were leaving. Like she'd taken a wrong turn and she didn't know how to get back. I wish I could have done something to help her. To stop Ma from leaving that day.

I wish there was something I could do now to make Ma go back.

FORTIFICATION

Christmas was over a week ago and everyone has gone back to work. I'm sitting in the shadow of the door. Ma is on the bottom step.

'Spare change?'

No one is giving her anything. I don't blame them. She looks like a corpse these days.

'Stingy git.' Ma spits at a guy who is passing.

Her hands are shaking real bad. She curses as someone else passes. Then she stands up and shoves her hands in her pockets. 'This is poxy. I'm going somewhere else.'

'Where?'

'I dunno. Maybe over by the river.'

'There's no use, Ma. There'll be no one there this time of day.' The bridge over the river was where we always used to beg. But I don't want Ma to go out. I don't want her to leave me on my own, not any more. 'What if the Authorities come back and you're not here?'

'They won't,' she says. 'Just wait here, will ye? I'll only be gone for a little bit.'

'They said after Christmas, Ma. They're going to come back.'

She's not listening, though. All she says is, 'Don't go out there, ye hear me?' Then she starts walking down the street.

'Ma!' I call. But there's no point. I watch till she disappears around the corner and then I go inside and lock the door.

Maybe I'll paint the third floor too, this time with pictures of Boat Woman and Glass Woman and Red Coat. I'll do one picture of them when it's sunny and they are happy. Though I don't think Glass Woman is ever happy. Then I'll do another one when they are sad and it's raining, like it is now.

I stop. It's not raining. I was just outside. And it wasn't raining. But I can hear a tinkling noise. Like rain hitting off Caretaker's tin roof.

I go back to the door and open it and peer out. It's not raining.

I close the door and listen. But whatever it was, it has stopped now.

'Rose?' I whisper. I watch the fingers of light that come through the gaps in the boards. But the dust is just normal boring dust. It's not doing anything.

'I'm not afraid of ghosts,' I say out loud in case anyone is listening. Or anything.

And it's true. I'm not.

But I am afraid of the Authorities. What if they come back and I'm on my own? What if I don't even hear them come in and they come straight into my bedroom at night or something?

I look over my shoulder at the door. That's how the Authorities will get in if they come. So I need to know when that door is opened.

I need an alarm.

I drag two bags of empty beer cans from the backyard into the kitchen. I tear a big hole in both. I pour them onto the floor. A little brown pool of liquid forms. It stinks of stale beer and cigarettes.

First I pick out the cans that have cigarette butts inside them and I throw them back into the ripped bags and chuck them out into the backyard. Then I put all the rest of the empty cans into a bucket and carry them outside. I wash them, and my fingers go blue from the cold and I have to stick them in my mouth till they've warmed up and I can feel them again.

And I suddenly have the flash. The piece of memory. The annoying feeling that there's something I've forgotten.

I blink and look at the sky. But I can't grab it, the memory. It's like something in the canal floating past just out of reach.

I shove my hands under my armpits and I wander around the backyard. I kick over a stone and some rubbish and bricks till I find what I'm looking for. A rusty nail. Then I pick up a flat stone that's rounded at the edges so it won't hurt to hold it.

The final thing I need is some wire. I think about every floor of the mill and in my mind I go through all the things that are lying on the ground or sticking out of the ceiling till I can think of where I'd find some. The sixth floor.

I run up the stairs to the sixth floor and I sidestep along the wall and then crawl across the rotted floorboards till I get to the massive corkscrew grinder that's hanging over the hole. There are loads of wires coming out of it. Some of them reach up to the ceiling. Some are fat and some are skinny. It's the skinny ones that I want.

I stand beside the bin under the chute that comes from the conveyor belt. I hold onto the edge of the bin with one hand and I stand on my tippy-toes and stretch up real tall till I can wrap my fingers around the skinniest of the wires. I yank it and it gives, so I pull more and more and the wire's falling down all around me.

It's three or four times the length of me. I bend it at the same point, from one side to the other, till it snaps.

I need a little more.

I reach up and grab a second wire. It looks pretty loose. I yank on it but it's jammed. I wrap both my hands around it and I pull real hard and it comes flying down. But there's this rumble and a 'snap' from the roof and the corkscrew drops down with a jerk. I think it's going to fall through the floor. It swings a little. I grab the side of the bin. I hold my breath. I wait till it calms down.

I think that's enough wire. I probably shouldn't do it again.

I go back down to the kitchen.

I pick up the rusted nail and the flat stone and the first can. I start to hammer the nail into the bottom of the can till it punctures it. I do the same with the next.

It takes me the whole morning to do every can, but then I have over a hundred of them with holes in the bottom.

I break off pieces of wire and feed them in through the bottom of the cans and out through the top. I do that again and again till I have ten rows of cans all tied together. At one end I make a hook with the leftover wire so that it looks like a clothes hanger opened out.

I take the rows and drag them into the basement. I look around the floor and find some pipe that's just the right size. I hook the rows of cans over the pipe.

Now I go back to the kitchen and grab a chair. I carry the pipe with the cans in one hand and the chair in the other, all the way over to the front door.

I stand on the chair and lift up the pipe and I balance it on the ledge above the door. I climb down and move the chair and unlock the door and open it real fast. The door hits the cans and the whole thing falls to the floor. There's a loud clatter.

Now there's no way the Authorities can come through the front door without me hearing them.

I'm pretty happy that my plan works. I go to shut the front door so I can lift the pipe back up again but then I stop.

It's real busy outside. Everyone's back at work and it's lunchtime and there are people walking up and down. I look at the floor inside the door. Ma left one of her old begging cups. I pick it up. It's empty.

I wonder if she's out there somewhere right now with a cup in front of her, saying 'Spare change?' to people who don't care. I hope that's what she's doing.

I step out and pull the door behind me but I don't close it. I sit down in the shadows and watch the people go past. I look at the spot where Ma was sitting earlier. It's only three steps away. But it's outside.

I push myself up and crab-walk out, inch by inch, till I can slip onto the bottom step. Two guys walk past, chatting away. A woman in high heels and business clothes is coming. She's holding a sandwich that's all wrapped up in paper. She's fingering her change. If Ma was here she'd definitely get it off her, cos the woman can't pretend she doesn't have any when it's obvious she does.

She's almost at the steps now. Ma would ask her for spare change and the woman would look around and maybe say something like, 'Cold today, isn't it?' when she was dropping the coins in the cup. Ma would say 'thanks' and the woman might even smile at her before she left.

I take a deep breath. She's at the steps now. All I need to say is 'Spare change?' She's so close I could spit on her. I smell her perfume. Two words. That's all I need to say. I open my mouth. Try to speak. But I can't make the words come out. My breathing has gone all jaggedy.

She's passing the steps. She's putting the change in her pocket. Pulling her jacket tight.

I still don't say anything.

There are more people coming. She moves to the side. She walks past them. She's gone.

I grab the step behind me and pull myself up and scramble a little till I'm at the top, in the corner, in the shadows. I close my eyes and count to ten and try to stop my heart from racing.

There's no point. I can't do it. I can't go out there again. I can't say 'Spare change?'

I stand up and go back inside and shut the door.

US AND THEM

I had always seen people begging on the streets. The guy with the straggly beard who sat beneath the cash machine. The woman with the baby that never cried, begging outside the place where they sold theatre tickets.

I just didn't know we were like them.

Ma chose a bridge over the river cos that way we could see the Authorities coming a mile off in any direction. When we saw them I'd hop up and walk away into the crowd. Not too far. Just far enough so Ma could always see me but they wouldn't notice me.

We had to get up real early or else we'd wait till the offices closed, cos they were the best times for begging. Morning and evening. When people were off to work or going back home.

When Ma had enough money we went to get food. The Do-gooders had a centre where they handed it out. I'd have to stand outside while Ma queued. That meant they'd only give her food for one person but she was never hungry back then. Not for food anyway.

Friday was wash day cos that's when the Do-gooders handed out clean clothes. We'd choose a pub or café we'd never been in before and we'd go into the jacks and wash real quick and change into the new clothes before the security guard could chuck us out.

Everywhere Ma went, I went. If she was sleeping in the morning, I'd play in the trees and pretend that the shed was a ruined castle and I was a princess wandering through the forest. And when she went to Monkey Man's gate, I went with her and hid behind her.

I hated going there. But at least he didn't know where we lived. No one did. It was ours. But then one day we came back, and before we even got inside we could hear the voices. And I saw a flash of neon yellow. And Ma cursed. And I knew the shed wasn't ours any more.

We grabbed Ma's rucksack from behind the bush and we legged it through the trees and under the archway and back onto the streets.

A BULLET WAITING TO
BE FIRED

I'm walking up the stairs when I hear something from way off. I know the noise but I can't place it straight away. I'm sure it means something. And then I know what it is and I'm flying back down the stairs. It's my beer-can alarm!

It must be Ma. She's back. That's all. It's okay.

I'm running downstairs so fast that I nearly fall into the basement, but I make myself slow down and on the bottom step I take a deep breath and I stick my head around the corner.

I see them. Men in plastic hats. And yellow jackets. Coming through the door.

The Authorities are here.

A nest of spiders explodes inside me.

The Authorities. They're going to take me away and I'll lose everything. I'll never see Ma again. They'll steal my home. I have to stop them but I don't know what to do.

But there's one thing I do know.

Everyone's afraid of ghosts.

I grab my bicycle and lift it up the stairs. At the next floor, I leave it by the stairs and I tiptoe into the room, past all of the dead machines, down to the other end. I start picking up the bowling pins. When all ten are standing in a triangle, I pick up the foam bowling ball and I return through the room. I grab a long piece of pipe and shove it under my arm and I'm back on the stairs.

I place the bowling ball here in the stairway. Then I carry the pipe and the bicycle up to the next floor and I leave them in the classroom, and I go into the big room, picking up pieces of metal and brick and glass and broken board and pipe and anything else I can find. I put them beside the open funnels. Then I'm back out the door and up the stairs to the next floor, and I cross the rotted boards and crawl across the pipe to the periscope and shove my ear against it.

'. . . underground car park . . .' I hear someone say.

Another man with a deeper voice says, 'Personally I think the whole thing should be apartments—'

'Which,' interrupts the first voice, 'is why you've never been invited to a planning meeting, Bob.' They all laugh.

'Anyway! From the drawings, gentlemen, you can see . . . the shops and . . . here and here . . . and now, if you'd like to follow me upstairs . . .'

I jump up and run down one flight. Their feet are pounding on the stairs. They are coming up.

206

I wait just out of sight of the stairs till I hear them go into the second-floor room with the dead machines. Then I come down, real quiet.

I stay close to the wall opposite the bedroom. I pick up the foam bowling ball and stand with my back to the wall. I hear the boards creak and I know they are walking over to the windows at the other side.

'... six apartments per floor ... Highest spec. So, Oly, my friend, no scrimping on the fire insulation!'

He thinks he's hilarious. All the other men laugh. I peek real careful around the corner. They're all looking at the glass office building across the road. Their backs are to me.

I take a deep breath. Step forwards into the doorway. Aim at the plastic bowling pins, slightly to the right. Wind my arm. And then roll the ball as hard as I can.

I jump back behind the wall and wait a few seconds. Then there's a crash and I know I've scored a strike.

'Jesus!' the man with the deep voice says.

'My heart!' another says.

And then the one who thinks he's hilarious says, 'Ah, just some plastic pins. Obviously seen its share of squatters. Possibly the sporting kind.' They all laugh. 'Must have been the wind. Anyway, as I was saying ...'

I hear them wandering through the room again. After a minute, I risk another look. They are standing by the last machine, right under a pipe. I jump back behind the wall and run upstairs to the classroom and into the big room. I sprint past the funnels till I reach the fifth one.

207

I pick up a brick. Open the lid. Chuck it down.

I hear a yell.

I run straight to the fourth funnel and put my ear to it and I wait. There's talking and groaning. After ages I hear the men start to move and I think they are coming close to the fourth machine. I open the mouth of the funnel and I count to three and drop a piece of glass down. When I hear a scream, I know they're right below me, so I throw a brick down after it too.

Now there's more shuffling and groaning and I think they are leaving, so I run to the next funnel and throw a brick down it but I hear it crash off the ground below. At the next funnel, when I throw a metal bar down, I hear another roar, and I know I got another strike.

I run out of the room and grab the bicycle and line it up on the stairs. I hear the men coming close to the door below me. I know they are right there, just out of sight.

'Bloody deathtrap,' one of the men says.

'Health-and-safety nightmare,' the one with the deep voice says.

I see a shoe appear. I let go of the bicycle and jump behind the wall. I hear it roll and bounce and clatter and I hear a man shout, '*Move!*'

There is the sound of shuffling and grunting as the bicycle ploughs into them.

'What in the bloody hell is going on here?'

I don't wait. I grab the long piece of pipe that I left leaning against the wall. I sprint as fast as I can up to the sixth-floor room with the massive corkscrew. I run on my tippy-toes along the boards by the wall, and I crawl on my hands and knees across to the centre, right up to the massive corkscrew. I bring the pipe up over my head and I swing it as hard as I can, down on one of the bars that is holding the corkscrew in the air.

There is a loud dong. My hands sting from the shock, but the corkscrew sways. I smack it again. It jerks and the wires move. I smack it again and the whole room creaks. I hit it one more time and I hear something tearing and I take a step backwards. The ceiling dips. Cracks run across it like a spider's web. I take a few more steps back. There is another tearing sound. The corkscrew shakes. I'm crawling backwards and I grab the wall just as the ceiling breaks. It loses its grip on the wires and they all snap and the corkscrew plummets straight down, right through the floor.

I'm already running back towards the door when I hear it crash into the next floor. It tears the wood open and there is another crash. It must have gone through to the fourth floor! It crashes again and again and again and then the whole mill is shaking.

I'm sprinting down the stairs. The corkscrew has completely destroyed everything. At the fourth floor the periscope has vanished and there's only a hole there now. On the third floor there are three funnels left and a massive hole. On the second floor there is one machine missing and another one is sliding towards the hole in the middle.

I creep down to the basement and peek around. All four

men stand with their mouths wide open, staring at a gigantic corkscrew that has smashed into the concrete. The air tastes like stone.

One of them tilts his head back real slow till he's staring up, through the holes in every single floor, at the roof of the mill. They all do the same thing. They are covered in dust. One man's jacket is ripped. The other one has a bloody hand.

'My God,' the man who thought he was hilarious says.

'Once is bad luck,' the man with the deep voice says. 'Twice is a sign. This –' he waves a hand – 'this is an act of God. Or nature. Or whatever you want to call it. I don't care. It's a threat. And I, for one, am getting out of here.'

'My God,' the hilarious man says again.

The man with the deep voice starts to walk real quick towards the door and all the other men turn and run after him. They are holding their hats tight against their heads.

They're leaving! It worked! They're leaving! I throw my arms up in the air and I spin around and I'm dead happy.

But a man steps out from the kitchen and I freeze. He's right there. Right in front of me. I don't even drop my hands. It's too late to hide. He's going to grab me.

'What in the name ... ?' he says, but he's not looking at me. He walks like he's in a dream, right past me. He never looks at me. He stares at the mess that used to be the ceiling. And then he runs for the front door.

He didn't even see me.

THE ALLEYWAY

I had thought that the shed was the worst place we would ever stay. I was wrong.

We slept in loads of different places after we left the shed and none of them were good. The night before we found the mill we were in one of our spots. It was in a quiet alleyway that ran between two streets. There was a doorway where we could hide in the shadows and not be seen as long as we slept close together, which was fine cos by then it was the middle of winter and it was real cold.

We had hardly eaten all day and Ma totally forgot to go find food for me. But Ma couldn't remember anything that day. That day, she could hardly speak. She was just waiting till she had enough coins so she could buy what she needed and then we went back to the doorway in the alley.

Our sleeping bags had got wet a few nights before and they hadn't dried, and I hadn't eaten anything all day except for a sausage roll that I'd seen someone chuck in the bin that morning, which was hours and hours ago.

I told Ma I was hungry but she didn't listen to me. Instead she fell back into that doorway, and I turned away cos I didn't want to watch her eyes go all empty and I didn't want her to see me cry. That night she wouldn't have cared anyway and that would have made it even worse.

After a while, she went all limp like she always did. But my stomach hurt. I knew I wasn't supposed to leave her, especially at night cos anyone could grab me at night, not just the Authorities who were always looking for me, but anyone at all, a total stranger, and if they took me, Ma wouldn't have a notion where to find me. I knew that.

But I was so cold and so hungry. So I went out to the street to see if anyone else had thrown their food into a bin, just cos they didn't like it.

There was no one on the street. It was too cold. I reckoned everyone was probably inside watching TV and eating eggs and chips, cos that's what I'd be doing if I wasn't me. I remember my breath made clouds in the air and my fingers stung real bad. And I pretended my breath-clouds made an invisible cloak around me that kept me safe.

I walked away from the alley and down the street to the walls of the university. I kept close to the wall and I had to run between the patches on the path where the street lights stole away my invisibility. I walked slower through the dark patches.

I stopped when I could see the big gates to the university.

There was a massive stone arch there, with doorways and sheltered parts. It was a place where you'd always find people sleeping with their cardboard boxes beneath them and their sleeping bags around them and their bags under their heads so no one could take them. I even recognized one man. He was tall and looked like, even if you fed him for a year, he'd still be all bones and shadows.

There were two people with him that were wearing gloves and hats and heavy jackets. One was carrying this big box with a strap that went over his shoulder while the other, who I think was a woman, scooped out soup in a cup and handed it to the bony man. I could see the steam rising from the cup even from where I was standing and that was worse than having no food at all.

I wanted to go up and ask for a cup real bad, but I knew I couldn't.

So I didn't move, I just stood there and watched and listened to my stomach rumble. I saw a copper come up and talk to the Do-gooders and look all around him and then walk off, and I knew Ma was right – that the Do-gooders were spies for the police and nowhere was safe, especially at night, and I wanted to cry. All I wanted was some soup.

'You all right?' someone said, and I nearly jumped out of my skin with fright. I hadn't even noticed a man and woman walk up right beside me, and I was about to run till I saw her face. She was real tall, much taller than him, and she was dressed in high shoes. I could see her legs, which meant she must have been wearing a dress, but I couldn't see it cos she had a long red jacket on. But she wasn't looking at me. She was watching the Do-gooders and she seemed bored, and I knew that the man wasn't going to hurt me, cos he was with the woman and she just wanted to get to wherever they were going. So I didn't run.

'Freezing, isn't it? Must be twenty degrees. Or even less,' he said in this weird accent, and he looked at the Do-gooders for a while. 'You on your own?' he asked.

I answered, 'No,' real quick.

But then he said, 'Hungry?' And I couldn't say anything.

He lifted a paper bag and opened it up and pulled out a burger. It wasn't even open, it was still in the paper box. He held it out. 'Bought it for my friend,' he said. 'But he's gone off somewhere. Have it, if you want. I'm stuffed.'

And I did want it real bad, so I took it and he said, 'Okay, see you later,' and they went off down the road. When I took it out, it was big and round, and it was one of those ones with two burgers between the buns, and it was still warm and everything so I ate it right up, the whole thing, standing there by the wall. And I only thought about keeping some for Ma when it was all gone, and then I felt real bad so I ran back.

I went straight to the doorway and pulled my sleeping bag around me and I didn't say anything to Ma. I just rolled myself up as tight as I could and went to sleep.

But I woke up cos it got real cold. So cold that I went all numb and I couldn't feel anything. I rolled over to try to get close to Ma, and that's when I realized. She wasn't there.

214

I was sure she'd been there when I got back, but she wasn't there now.

And I got real scared cos what if she'd been taken away and locked up and I hadn't even noticed she was gone and that was hours and hours ago? What if whoever took her came back for me and took me away into Care and she never found me again? But I couldn't think of anything to do. So I lay there and waited.

I remember I was shaking cos I was real scared and real cold. But it got colder and colder, and the night went on for so long that I thought that maybe I'd just imagined the burger.

Then, from far off, I heard a siren wailing. It got closer. And closer.

Blue lights were bouncing off the walls of the alleyway. Yellow Jackets were jumping out of a van. Coming for me.

I sprang up. Slipped out. Sprinted real quiet down the alleyway.

I hid in the next doorway.

I peeped around the corner and saw them stop by our stuff and crouch down. I thought the burger man must have told them about me and when they saw I wasn't there they would start looking for me, so I stood as straight as I could and tried to become invisible.

It must have worked. Cos they never found me.

But I remember them lifting something up onto this tray that was so big, it took two men to carry it between them. There was a blanket on the tray. But it wasn't a blanket, not like Caretaker's. It was a black rubber sheet.

There were Yellow Jackets everywhere. Too many. I couldn't escape.

But then Ma was there.

Through the blue and the yellow she came. She took me by the hand. And we walked away. Away from the Authorities.

ANCIENT HISTORY

I'm lying on my mattress but I can't sleep. Ma said she was going begging on the bridge. But she never came home. Loads of times in the last few weeks she's come back late. But she's never not come back.

The mill feels different. Empty. With a huge hole in it that goes right through every floor from the top to the bottom. Like it has no heart. I roll over and pull the blankets around my chin.

It's a real windy night. I can hear the bridge whistling outside. The windows are rattling.

I hear something else, though. It's not the wind.

Shuffle, shuffle, shuffle . . .

I sit up straight and listen. Caretaker?

I can't tell where it's coming from. But I think it's close by. I get out of bed and open the door real quiet. I hear a creaking. It's coming from this floor, the one with the dead machines.

It's real dark and I don't want to run cos I can't tell where the hole starts, so I keep close to the wall till I get to the first window.

Shuffle, shuffle, shuffle . . .

'Caretaker?' I call.

There's a creaking sound, like someone trying to walk real quiet.

A gust of wind carries water from the canal, slaps it onto the window.

Thump, thump, thump.

It's on the stairs. I start moving back to the door, but the moon is shining through the broken window and I think I can see something in my room. A dark shadow. Big.

It's crossing the stairs. It's in here now. Between me and the door. It's coming towards me.

I try to call out but my breath is snatched away. It's too big. It can't be him. If it's not Caretaker, then . . .

I take a step backwards. It takes a step closer. I step back again but I trip up. I'm on the ground. I can't see anything now. Where is it? But then the shadow moves. It's even closer. I'm trapped.

I search the ground around me. There's nothing there to grab. I crawl back a bit more. I bump the wall. There's nowhere else to go. I want to run but I'll fall through the hole.

The shadow's real big and it's getting nearer.

I reach out. Search the ground. I only feel dirt. Then I find something. A brick? I wrap my fingers around it.

It comes closer. It's right over me. The light from the moon comes in through the window. The shadow has a face. And the face has a scar. And three eyebrows.

Monkey Man.

I scream.

He leans forwards. His arm comes out. He's going to grab me. I lift up the brick and swing it at his head as hard as I can and he stumbles to the side. I spring up and run. I can't see where I'm going and the floorboards creak, but he's right behind me so I run as fast as I've ever run.

I'm racing down the stairs. But there's someone else there, climbing towards me. It must be Scarecrow.

I turn and sprint upstairs, but I hear footsteps coming fast behind me. They're stronger than me and quicker than me and they're going to get me. I have to escape before they catch me but I'm running up, not down. And there's no other way out. I have to hide.

I get to the top of the stairs. The trapdoor!

I climb up onto the bricks, then onto the chair. I reach out to open the trapdoor but the chair slips. I fall backwards and I smack off the ground. I feel nothing but my heart roaring inside me.

I see him on the stairs below. And he sees me.

I jump up and run out onto the sky-bridge. The wind shoves me backwards. I push through it. The only way now is to go up onto the roof of the Silo but where do I go from there?

I hear him clanging across the sky-bridge. I clutch the ladder and start to climb. I won't make it, but there's nothing else I can do. My foot slips. I'm going to fall again. I'm dangling from the ladder. Something touches my foot. I scream and kick and I grip the ladder with all my strength. I look down.

There's no one grabbing me.

My arms are rattling out of their sockets and my heart has exploded and my eyes are squeezed shut.

I smell bin juice.

I find the step with my foot and I stand still for a second and breathe real hard. I look down. There's light from the moon on the canal, and it sweeps across the water and hits the mill and then it hits the sky-bridge. I see a bird's nest. And sunglasses with only one lens. And a long jacket and a hat.

I feel like a feather all blown to pieces, like the wind is going to just take me away and scatter me all over the city. I take a step down. Then another. I can smell bin juice and it's the best thing I've ever smelled.

'Caretaker?' I say. My voice sounds tiny. I go back down the few steps onto the sky-bridge.

'You're all right, kiddo,' he says. He's looking over the side of the bridge into the backyard. 'You're all right now.'

I don't think he's talking to me. *Someone just walked over my grave.*

'Is he dead?' I whisper. I look at the ground beneath the sky-bridge. But there's nothing there. The wind is howling but Caretaker says nothing. 'I don't get it,' I say. 'Where's Monkey Man and Scarecrow?'

He turns to me and the moon watches me through his one lens. 'Nothing chasing you, kiddo. Just your own past catching up on you.'

There's no Monkey Man.

Caretaker turns back again. 'She fell,' he says.

'Who?'

'My Rose.' Caretaker's not looking at the ground. He's looking at some place that's real far away. 'She fell.'

'*Your* Rose?'

And I remember him saying it was all his fault. That's his secret. 'She fell,' I say. 'She was your kid. And she fell.'

'Should've been watching out for her.' He sighs and he looks at his hands. 'They were going to close the mill. I'd been moaning about losing my job for weeks. But when the time came, I helped them. I locked up all the doors and turned off the machines and watched to make sure all the millers left. Too busy watching. Didn't notice she wasn't with me.

'She used to come to the mill to play and we'd walk home together when I finished work.' Caretaker cranes his head back and looks at the Silo roof. 'She liked going up there, even though I told her, time and again, to keep away from it. Must've come up one last time. Door was locked. I know – I'd locked it. Must've crawled up through that trapdoor and onto the conveyor belt and out over here.' He points to the empty night right above our heads. 'Slipped.'

I stare down at the couch and imagine what Caretaker saw the day he came up here and found her. I shiver. Then I remember something else.

'The coins?' I say and now he looks at me and he smiles like he's remembering. 'Industrious little one. The millers would pay her to clean the flour away after their shifts. Meant they could leave a few minutes earlier and she was here anyway, waiting for me. Every Saturday they'd pay her. Leave the coins out for her to collect. She must have been there when I turned off the machines. Hiding. But she never collected the coins that last day. She ran up here instead.'

He looks me. 'She was my only child. My world. And the day she died, my world crumbled.'

'Forty-seven years ago,' I say.

Caretaker nods. 'Forty-seven years ago she died and I've been here ever since.'

He's turning something around in his hand. It's a coin.

'But time moves on whether you like it or not. And so must we.' Caretaker smiles at me. 'Rose isn't here any more.'

He lifts his hand and tosses the coin over the edge. The moon catches it as it falls. Then Caretaker blows a kiss to the wind and he turns and shuffles away.

CRUMBLING CASTLE

I must have fallen asleep. I open my eyes. It's morning. I turn over.

Ma's still not back.

I sit up. I hurt all over, like it was me who fell and not . . .

I want to cry. It's stupid. But I feel bad. Even though Rose's life and death were washed away a long time ago.

There's a sound and I remember last night and already my heart starts pounding again, even though I know Monkey Man wasn't really here.

But it's not inside the mill. It's from outside. It's the usual sound of the city but it feels real close. I jump up and pull down the mattresses from where I shoved them against the door.

I listen. I hear cars revving and people shouting and a cat meowing and a seagull squawking, and some banging and clattering, like I always hear. But the banging sounds are closer now. I open the door real slow.

Across the hall there's the huge hole and half the floor is gone. The boards are snapped and they bend downward. I hug the wall and I reach the window and look down.

Men in plastic hats and yellow jackets! Everywhere. They're all around the building. They've come back!

Where is Ma?

Half the street is closed off. The traffic is only driving on one side now. There are two, three, four vans, and the men in the yellow jackets are taking huge pieces of board out of them. I push my face real tight against the window. I can't see straight down, but over to the side I can see where they are going with the boards. They are linking the boards together. They're building a fence around the Castle!

Something is reflecting in the glass of the office building across the road. There are two Yellow Jackets and they are sticking something to the fence. I can't see what it is, they're in the way, but they finish and walk away, and now I can read it, even though it's backwards. It says,

DANGER
CONSTRUCTION SITE
DO NOT ENTER

I look left and right out the window and see nothing, but I move to the next window and shove my face against it and look to the right, up the street.

'No!'

A big red crane is bent over in prayer outside the Silo. It's grinning. And it's hungry.

'Ma,' I whisper. 'Where are you?'

I turn and leg it out of the room and up, up, up till I'm on the roof.

The clock on the church says 8.53. I grab the binoculars. She *has* to be coming back. She just has to.

I search the streets. The paths, the office buildings and the cafés. I don't see her. I see Red Coat. She's walking to her office. A car stops beside her. Short Guy jumps out. He's running. Shouting. She turns. Sees him. But she's angry. He grabs her hand. She snatches it back and walks away. Behind her, he drops to one knee. He calls out to her and he holds something. She stops. Listens.

He's holding a box. He's talking. Her shoulders fall. She turns a bit. Then a bit more. She can see the box now too. She takes a step back. Then another. He holds up the box. She opens the lid. Lifts out something. A book.

Ulysses.

Then all of a sudden I get the flash of memory. The rubber blanket. I squeeze my eyes shut. I'm back in the alleyway. I leave Ma to go look for food. I'm moving from street light to street light. I'm outside the university. A man and a woman stop. He's short and she's tall and he gives me a burger.

'It was him,' I say. 'Short Guy. He gave me the burger that night.'

But then I'm back in the alleyway and the air is so cold it stings my nose. I feel the cold go through me, fill me up.

225

I open my eyes. I have to find Ma. I search the street but she's not down there.

I sprint to the other side of the roof. I look at the bridge and the road that runs along beside the canal. I don't see her.

Where are you, Ma?

I see something else, though. The green boat. It's moving. The woman stands outside, at the back of the boat. She's driving it. The baby is strapped to her and there's an orange life jacket wrapped around them both.

The canal is still. The reflection of the clouds and the buildings sits inside it, like there's another world beneath the water. The boat pulls away from the bank and ripples the underwater world.

Behind it are two swans. There's no baby with them now. It must have finally flown away.

I sweep the binoculars high to the top floor of the apartment building. Glass Woman has moved a chair to face the window. She's sitting there all alone. She's holding one of those tall skinny glasses full of wine, even though it's early. She takes a gulp. Stares out the window like she's looking straight at me. But she doesn't see me.

In the next room the kid sits and stares out the window too. There are Lego blocks on the floor but she's not building anything.

I look back at her ma. Then her. They look the same. Their eyes are empty.

I lower the binoculars. Check the streets and the bridge and the canal bank. Where are you, Ma?

Behind me I hear a screech. Metal yawning. I drop the binoculars. I turn.

The mantis is rising. Its shadow moves over the roof. The sun winks off it. It's ready.

Where's Ma?

I run back to the other side of the roof and I'm wishing so hard that she'll be down there. She's not.

Short Guy is standing in front of Red Coat. He's begging her, I can see it in his eyes. She drops her handbag. She's speaking now. I'm not sure, but I think she says, 'Yes, I will, yes.'

I take one last look up and down the street. But Ma's not there.

I turn and I run. Across the roof and beneath the arm of the crane and down the ladder and over the sky-bridge and down through the mill and into the basement. When I get to Caretaker's window, I jump up and stick my head out.

His blankets are gone.

'Caretaker!'

I can't see the feet passing on the street above any more, cos the Yellow Jackets have almost finished building the fence. It goes right along the street where Caretaker used to sell his books. There's only a small gap now, where the ramp out of Caretaker's place meets the road.

There aren't any men in yellow jackets out there, so I squeeze my head and shoulders through the gap till I'm half out the window, and now I can see him.

He's standing beside two towers of blankets. They're all

folded up. And his books are all stacked up against the wall too.

'Caretaker! What are you doing?' I want to jump down and kick his books and push over his blanket tower. But he doesn't look at me. He keeps shuffling around. He picks up a few blankets and puts them into a shopping trolley. Then he picks up some books and puts them into the trolley too.

'Caretaker!' I shout but he's ignoring me. He takes one book and shakes his head and puts it on top of the pile by the wall. I drag myself out through the window and jump down onto the ground. I take his sleeve and I force him to look at me.

'What are you doing? You can't leave. You have to help me find Ma,' I say.

But all he says is, 'Come on now, kiddo. Let me go.'

'They put up a sign,' I say. 'It says Do Not Enter.'

I want him to tell me what I know isn't true. That they are going to leave us alone.

He looks at me and smiles, but it's not a happy smile, it's one of those sad smiles. 'They're tearing it down, whether you like it or not.'

'I can't leave,' I say. 'Ma's not back.' But he just shrugs and keeps putting books in his trolley. I grab a book out of his hand and throw it on the ground. '*Help* me, Caretaker!'

He doesn't get mad. He just nods and turns his back on the rest of his books and the blankets, as if he's finished with them anyway and he has enough. He puts his hands on the trolley.

'Don't, please?' I say, and I grab the side of the trolley so he can't move it.

'No choice,' he says. 'I gotta go. And so do you. Why don't you come with me, we'll walk out together?'

But I can't leave. I have to wait for Ma. Cos she'll be back. She always comes back.

'Please,' I say. 'Help me.'

Caretaker takes his hand away from the trolley. He looks at me like there are words on my face but they're all scrambled up. Then he tilts his head back and watches the mill.

'The coins,' he says. He crouches down in front of me and his jacket falls around him. 'The millers left the coins out for her on that last day. Like they always did. But she never got to collect them.' Caretaker sighs. 'When you left them out, I thought it was her leaving me a message. And I guess it was. In a way. Now I know Rose isn't here any more.'

He watches me for a while. 'You can't stay here. But trust me, there are better things for you than this.'

I shake my head. Why doesn't he understand?

'She has to let you go, you know?' he says. I think he means Ma. 'And I have to do the same.' He looks over my shoulder at the window. 'I gotta let her go.'

'But it's not the same!' I say.

'Yes,' he says, and he takes off his sunglasses. 'It is.'

I see his two eyes for the first time ever. The second one's brown too. It's almost the exact same as the other. But it has little gold flecks in it, which makes it look more, I dunno, alive or something.

'Rose,' he says.

The way he says it, it's like it's a full stop.

He breathes in real deep and then lets it out. 'Years I've waited. For what?' He looks up at our Castle again. 'For her to forgive me. But she already had. It's me that has to move on.'

He folds his sunglasses and he puts them down, real gentle, on the ground. 'I'm old now,' he says. 'Spent a lifetime here. But I think I'll go while the sun is still shining.'

He stands with a groan like an old tree pulling out its roots. He puts his hands back on the trolley.

'Let her go,' he says. 'Nothing chasing you. Nothing holding you here. Nothing to be scared of. It's just time to move on, that's all.'

I can't believe he's leaving.

'Why won't you help me, Caretaker?'

Caretaker smiles at me. 'Cos it's up to you now.' He looks at me the same way Ma does when she's waiting for me to figure out the Moral. He nods. Then he starts to push the trolley up the ramp and onto the street. And then he's gone.

A SECRET ESCAPE ROUTE

I jump back through the window and sprint all the way over to the front door. Even though I'm scared they'll see me, I open it and look out. There's only one gap left in the fence. It's at the bottom of the steps, just in front of the spot where Ma usually begs.

Traffic is crawling by and there are Yellow Jackets scurrying past the gap. I hide behind the boards and take a few deep breaths.

I stick my head out through the opening. I see a few people but none of them are Ma. Then a man in a yellow jacket comes towards me and I dart behind the boards again.

She's coming back. She has to be.

I hear Caretaker's voice. *It's up to you now.*

And that feeling comes again. The feeling that there's something I should be worried about and I don't know what it is.

Except suddenly I do.

The thing that's been annoying me all this time. It's that I don't remember how we got here.

I mean, I remember that night in the alley. I remember I ran and hid in the next doorway when the Yellow Jackets came. I stood as straight as I could and tried to stay invisible. And they never found me.

But I don't remember how we got here. To the Castle.

I remember them lifting something up onto that tray. It took two men to carry it between them. I know there was a blanket on the tray. But it wasn't a blanket, not like Caretaker's. It was a black rubber sheet. And there was something else. A hand. There was a hand sticking out of the rubber sheet.

But then Ma pushed through the blue and the yellow. She found me. And we walked away from the lights. Into the darkness. We were invisible again.

And when we were far away from that alley, she knelt down in front of me and held my hand, and said, 'I'm so sorry. I woke up and you weren't there. I went to find you. But I shouldn't have. I should've stayed and waited for you.'

I told her it was all right cos she came back.

She was crying then, and she said in this shaking voice, 'We'll go find that Castle then, yeah?'

And I said, 'Yeah. One with a moat and a drawbridge and a secret escape route.'

'Just you and me,' she said.

I remember all that. But I don't remember how we got here.

And now I see Ma's face again. That night. But this time it's different. It's flashing blue in the light from the van. And it's crushed. Crumpled. She's crying.

And I remember something else. I remember being lifted. The van doors were closing. The blue lights were fading as the gap got smaller and smaller till there was nothing left. Nothing and no one. Just me and the darkness.

I was in that van.

I open my eyes. People are walking past the gap in the fence. They glance at the mill as they pass. They don't see me.

I lift my hand. Stick it out of the gap. A woman walks past. She must think it's weird, this hand sticking out of the gap. But she doesn't notice it.

'I was in that van,' I whisper.

Ma couldn't have walked away with me cos there were too many Yellow Jackets. And they put a rubber blanket over me. They lifted me up. They put me in the van and took me with them.

I was on the tray. It was me.

I know it's true. Cos I've always known it. Somewhere inside, I knew.

I take a deep breath. I drop my hand. I turn round and see the stones of the mill. I look up at the Silo roof and imagine I can see me looking back down.

It's just a story, the Castle. A fairy tale.

I turn back. Look out of the gap. And I see her. Ma. She's coming back.

Her hair is wild and she's flying towards me and she looks just like she did in the alleyway that night. Wrecked. Scared. And sorry.

'You came back,' I say before she reaches me.

She stops. She's out of breath but she looks real happy that she made it back just in the nick of time. 'I'm sorry, love,' she says. 'I'm so sorry.' She kneels down in front of me and she smiles. Her hand stretches out. She's reaching for me. To hold my hand. To take me with her. 'Come on, love, we have to go.'

I kneel down too. But I don't take her hand.

'Where?' I ask.

And I know what she's going to say cos I've heard the words before. Cos this has all happened before.

'Anywhere you want, love. Anywhere. I promise.'

I feel a hole open up inside me. 'A castle?' I say.

'Yeah.'

'Just the two of us?' I say.

'Yeah.'

I nod. 'You came back, Ma.'

"Course, ye eejit. I'd never leave you.'

And the hole inside me aches cos I know it's true. 'You came back, Ma. I know ye did.' I pause till I'm sure she's listening. 'I saw ye. That night in the alleyway.'

Ma's smile melts away. 'No,' she whispers.

'Yeah,' I say.

Ma's eyes are going all deep. And I know what it means. But this time I can't let her drown.

'I left you that night,' I say. 'I wasn't supposed to. But I went to look for food. And you woke up. And I wasn't there. So you went looking for me. But you couldn't find me. Then you came back.'

She nods. 'I came back.'

'I know. But it was too late, Ma. I was already gone.'

Two Yellow Jackets come up to the gap in the fence. They're holding a board. The last board to finish the fence. They see Ma. But they don't see me. 'Ah here, come on! It's time to go,' one of them shouts. 'Bloody squatter.' He shakes his head. But the men drop the board and leave.

Ma doesn't even notice them. She's staring at me like she wants me to make it all better. So I say, 'You're not stuck here cos of the Authorities, Ma. The Authorities aren't even after us. You're stuck here cos of that night.'

Ma shakes her head. She covers her mouth with her hand. She's going to cry.

'But you kept your promise,' I say. 'You found us a castle. And it was good, Ma. It was.'

Ma nods.

'It just got bad cos we got stuck here. That's all,' I say. 'Now it's time to go.'

She looks up at the mill and shakes her head. 'No. I can't. I won't leave you.'

'You have to leave, Ma. I'll leave too.' I say.

'You'll come with me?'

I look at the ground for a bit. I roll some grit under my

fingers. 'You know what, Ma? Every castle has a secret escape route.'

When I look up, Ma's face has gone all soft. Like Gran's mushroom face.

'Yeah?' she says.

'Yeah,' I say and I point to the gap. Ma turns and looks at the traffic passing by.

'Not much of a secret, love,' Ma says.

'Nah, that's not it. The secret escape route's not a place. It's a way.'

Ma crawls forwards a bit so she's closer to me.

'What is it? What's the secret?'

I smile. And she smiles back. And it's a real smile.

'Together. That's the secret way out, Ma. We have to leave together.'

Ma takes one of those breaths that makes her whole body shake.

'Please, Ma? Will you leave with me?'

Ma shakes her head.

'You said it was time to move on, Ma. You were right. But we can still leave together, can't we?'

She rubs her face with the palms of her hands. She takes a few shuddery breaths. Then she drops her arms.

'Where will you go?'

I look up at the sky. There's a break in the clouds. The sun's rays fan through. It looks like the fingers of a giant searching for souls, to take them out of this world.

'A castle. With halls and secret tunnels and a massive

garden. And rooms that have real curtains that hang all the way to the floor, and duvet covers that match. I'll keep a room for you, Ma. Beside mine and Rose's.'

Her eyebrows arch in a big question mark.

'She's Caretaker's girl. She likes castles too,' I say.

Ma smiles but she doesn't ask. And I don't tell. We both just sit there for a while and look at each other till I say, 'You got to do it, Ma. Not me.'

She grabs me and hugs me real tight. 'I miss you,' she says. 'I miss you so bloody much. And I love you. I'll never, ever stop missing you and I'll never, ever stop loving you.'

'I know,' I say.

Her tears are warm on my neck. I push her away and make her look at me.

'One thing, Ma. You have to promise me something first.'

'Anything, love.'

There's something different about her. She looks wrecked but her eyes, they're not drowning.

I know she's ready. So am I.

'You have to forgive her.'

'Who?'

'Gran.'

'What are you talking about?' she says.

'Sometimes you look at me with the same look Gran had the day we left. You have to forgive her.'

'But—'

'Don't you miss her?'

I've never asked her what happened with Gran. I think

that's why she doesn't know what to say right now. She's staring at me. But this time I stare right back. I don't blink and I don't look away. I don't ask her neither. Cos it doesn't matter now.

Ma looks down the street. In the direction that the school girls walk.

She nods. It's only a tiny nod. But it's a nod.

'Nothing's unforgivable, Ma.'

She bites her lip. A tear rolls down her cheek. She wipes it away. But more come.

'Promise me you'll go back to Gran's. That you'll get better. That you won't drown.'

Ma closes her eyes. She takes a deep breath. Then another. Then opens them and she nods again.

'Say it, Ma.'

'I promise.'

'Promise you promise?'

'Yeah, love. I do.'

And we both stay there for a while till I say, 'Look at the state of ye,' cos her face is all wet and runny.

Then she does this real goofy smile and she flicks her hair like she's pretending she looks gorgeous. I laugh.

'Nothing a few home-cooked meals can't fix,' she says. She takes my hand. This time I let her.

'And a hairbrush,' I say.

'And maybe some make-up,' she adds.

Ma stands and pulls me up. We look at the Castle.

'It was a poxy hole, in fairness,' she says.

'Nah,' I say. 'It was deadly.'

Ma smiles at me. She leans forwards till her forehead is touching mine. She holds it there a long time. Then she whispers, 'Ready?'

'Yeah,' I say. 'You?'

'Yeah,' she says.

'Sure?'

'Sure I'm sure.'

She takes her head away and kisses my forehead. She's still holding my hand when she turns. She steps through the gap of the fence. Then she looks at me and smiles.

She squeezes my hand real tight. I squeeze back.

And then I let go.

If anyone is watching, they might see a girl step out of the shadow of the mill, just as the Yellow Jackets close in. They'd see her leave behind the broken windows and weeds that grow in between the big stones. They'd see her step away from a Castle that's about to crumble and tumble into the canal and disappear like the memories of a ghost.

If anyone is watching, they'd see a girl take a deep breath and a step and then another, out of the gap in the fence and into the light and the noise and the traffic and the people.

If anyone is watching, they'd see. But no one sees me. I'm invisible.

Acknowledgements

A friend said to me that he imagined writing must be a very lonely occupation. I replied, not at all.

Of course I sit alone dreaming and writing and editing until I have something worth sharing. But once I do, there are a lot of people I rely on. People who assist, advise and encourage me.

I would like to acknowledge the Irish Writers Centre, a wonderful resource for Irish writers, and the place where I found direction and focus in the early days. Through the centre I joined the Children's and YA group, where I learned so much about the difference between good writing and a good novel. I would particularly like to thank Simone, Aoife, Aine and Colleen for their countless hours of editorial comments, advice, encouragement, tea and cakes.

Audrey, my very first fan, thank you for wading through every draft.

I can't possibly thank my agent, Claire Wilson, enough. Nothing in my career will ever be as exciting as the very first email I got from you. But since then, your insight and patience have been simply invaluable.

I'm not sure if it is unusual, but I love the editorial process. I took this book as far as I could myself, but Rachel and Lucy at Simon & Schuster, and Kathy at Penguin Random House, helped me to mould it into the best book it could be. Thank you so much for all your hard work and wisdom, and for accommodating the arrival of my daughter onto the scene, mid edit!

Finally, none of this would have been possible without your support and belief in me, Bob. Perhaps there are writers that find this to be a lonely occupation. But I will forever be grateful that while I may sometimes struggle, it's never alone.

Sarah Carroll currently splits her time between a houseboat in Ireland and travel abroad. She recently returned from five years in Tanzania, where she founded and ran a hostel while working to support local community projects. She continues to promote ethical overseas volunteering through her blogs and films while planning her next book. *The Girl in Between* is her debut novel.

Q&A with the author

What inspired you to write The Girl in Between?

Most of the locations we see in the novel exist (or existed). The mill was located across the water from where I live (it has since been mostly torn down). There was a homeless man living in its shadow. I'd see him sleeping there in the mornings, with people hurrying by him on their way to work.

One day, I looked at the mill and I thought to myself, there's a young girl trapped in there. Why? Because it's her refuge from life on the streets. The mill is her home and she shares it not only with her mother, but with the ghosts of the past.

That evening I wrote the first chapter.

So, really, the mill and the homeless man that lived beneath it inspired the story.

The Girl in Between explores the idea of homelessness, which is an issue many people in Ireland are experiencing. Did you want to bring attention to this?

I didn't begin the novel with the sole aim of highlighting the homelessness crisis in Dublin. Once I decided to write a story based in the mill, however, I immediately knew I would be dealing with themes of homelessness and grief.

I wanted to explore the meaning of home to a child that didn't have one, and to give a voice to someone so vulnerable yet brave. I wanted to know how a child, exposed to the horrors of living on the streets, could still find a way to be a child.

The ending – with its twist – is particularly shocking. Did you know when you started writing that the girl in the story was a ghost?

Yes! For me, the mill represents not only a castle, but a limbo land – a facade of a crumbling past about to be replaced by an uncaring digital future. The girl, like the mill, embodies the past. She is stuck in the mill because she is stuck in limbo. And she is being kept there by grief, both her own and Ma's. I knew that for the story to end and the mill to be torn down, the girl must move on.

Have you always wanted to be a writer, and do you have more stories planned?

If you want to be a writer, you have to have more stories planned! I have a few novels in various stages of completion, but the next novel to be published is about a girl who discovers that the attics in her row of Georgian houses are connected. The main themes are bullying and the power of words.

To answer the first part of the question, no, I didn't always want to be a writer. I studied geology in university and after I worked in geophysics, then I travelled a lot, then I opened a hostel in Tanzania and ran that for a few years. Then I considered writing.

There was one night in Tanzania when I lay in bed, melting in the heat. I had just returned from a trip home, where it had been snowing, and as I lay there, I started dreaming of a land where it was always Christmas. The next day when I was jogging, I thought about it again. And the next. Soon, I realized I had a story I needed to write. So I wrote it. That was seven years ago.

What were your favourite books and authors growing up?

That's tough to answer because I read anything I found. But the ones that stuck with me were books that helped me to learn about the world outside of my own life. I remember devouring novels about social issues, like *Roll of Thunder, Hear My Cry*, and *Under the Hawthorn Tree* and *The Twelfth of July*. I always loved good comedy too. Basically anything ever written my Roald Dahl I adore, and (though I read it later in my teens) *The Hitchhiker's Guide to the Galaxy* is in my top three books of all time.

Lastly, is it true you live on a houseboat? What's that like?

Ha! Yes, I do, some of the time anyway. It's great, I love it. But it's small. And, with the arrival of our daughter, my family just got bigger. So we may not be on the boat much longer . . .

#HASHTAGREADS

Bringing the best YA your way

TOMMY WALLACH
MORGAN MATSON
ROBYN SCHNEIDER CASSANDRA CLARE
CLARE FURNISS
DARREN SHAN
C.J. FLOOD
STEPHEN CHBOSKY

HONOR & PERDITA CARGILL
SOPHIE MCKENZIE
AMY ALWARD
JENN BENNETT

#R

PAIGE TOON GAYLE FORMAN
BECCA FITZPATRICK
SCOTT WESTERFELD
S.J. KINCAID

Join us at **HashtagReads**,
home to your favourite YA authors

Follow us on Twitter
@HashtagReads

Find us on Facebook
HashtagReads

Join us on Tumblr
HashtagReads.tumblr.com